THE MADNESS OF LOVE

Mary Everest is plain, dowdy, and overlooked. When she finally kisses handsome Martin Hayle under the mistletoe, she's ecstatic. But then she overhears him admit to her sister Carol that he only kissed her out of pity, and her heart is broken. She runs away to France, determined to make her own way in the world and leave her family behind forever. Then the train she is travelling on crashes. Mary wakes in hospital — under the eye of the attractive Dr. Rhodes . . .

DENISE ROBINS

THE MADNESS OF LOVE

Complete and Unabridged

LINFORD
Leicester

First published in Great Britain in 1954

First Linford Edition
published 2022

A catalogue record for this book is available
from the British Library.

ISBN 978–1–4448–4776–5

Published by
Ulverscroft Limited
Anstey, Leicestershire

Printed and bound in Great Britain by
TJ Books Ltd., Padstow, Cornwall

This book is printed on acid-free paper

1

'Mary — Mary! I want you!'

Mary Everest, standing in the middle of her bedroom, just about to take off her overall and plunge into a hot bath, so sorely needed after the fatigue of a long day's work, paused in the act of unbuttoning the belt and clicked her tongue.

'Now what does Carol want?' she said aloud.

'Hurry, Mary!' came Carol Everest's voice from the bedroom downstairs.

'Mary, come and help me buckle these shoes — they're much too tight!' came another, more youthful voice from the room next door. That was Judy, Mary's youngest sister, aged seventeen.

Mary sighed. She would never be ready to receive the guests who were expected; she would be late for dinner, undoubtedly, if she had to assist both Carol and Judy before she started dressing herself. However, that did not matter. Probably she would not be missed if she were late. Nobody ever bothered about her.

'I'll come to you in a second, Judy!' she called out to the young girl next door. 'I must just run down and see what Carol wants.'

She pushed a lock of hair back from a rather flushed, grimy face, and clicked her tongue with annoyance once again as she regarded her dirty fingers. She was longing to get clean and put on that new frock that lay on her bed awaiting her . . . the prettiest frock she had had for years. She was so hoping that she would look nice to-night. Of course Carol and Judy would outshine her, they always did. They were both so pretty, so much more wordly-wise than she. Somehow she had managed to remain old-fashioned and badly dressed in spite of the money her father had made, and she had never been called pretty by her dearest friend. In fact, she was plain and she knew it.

But to-night, Christmas Eve, Martin Hayle was coming to dinner. Martin had been at school with Mary's brother, Jack, and was now just 'down' from Oxford. He was the one person in the world for whom Mary most wanted to shine. Ever since she had known him she had cherished a secret passionate love for him; first a schoolgirl's adoration, now the deeper, more serious affection of a woman of twenty-two.

'I *must* make myself attractive to Martin *somehow*!' she told herself pathetically as she ran down to her elder sister's room.

The Grange, Mary's home, was one of the biggest places in Dene Park, near Enfield, and the Everest girls the most popular. The life they led there was suburban, Dene Park being but a suburb. But Carol and Judy were constantly up in the West End with their friends and it seemed to Mary that they had reached the heights while she remained hopelessly dull and 'out of it.'

She helped the pretty Carol to dress, then went to Judy's room. How pretty she looked, she thought, in that mist-blue organdi dress. Judy danced to her dressing-table, seized a cigarette and lit it.

'We shall have some fun to-night,' she said, her blue eyes sparkling. 'Carol's got her beloved Martin, and I shall have Chris Miller — he's a wonderful dancer. Hope we'll get some good music on the radio, Mary.'

'Yes,' said Mary dully.

'Carol's got her beloved Martin!' Judy's careless words made her already drooping spirits sink to zero. She knew, of course, that Carol cared for Martin Hayle, but Martin had not yet asked her to marry him. He was not her possession. Must she monopolise him entirely to-night?

'You'll have to entertain Dad's pal — Mr. Cortright,' added Judy, laughing. 'He's just your style.'

These words, so carelessly cruel, uttered by a charming young girl to a plain elder sister, seemed to turn Mary for a moment from a quiet patient creature into a resentful fury.

'Mr. Cortright just my style? Oh, is he? Why should he be? He's fifty and bald and never opens his mouth except to stutter at Dad! Why should he be *my* style? Do you think just because I'm plain and can't dance that I haven't my longings, my wish to be gay and paid attention like you and Carol?'

She broke off, her face red, her eyes full of hot tears. Then with a choking sob she turned and rushed out of the room into her own, slamming the door behind her.

Judy stared after her with wide-open eyes. She had not meant to hurt her sister. But one got so used to thinking of 'old Mary' as the ugly duckling, better out of the way when one was having a good time. How could men like Chris Miller or Tom Sharron or any of the Dene Park crowd be expected to pay attention to funny, shy, plain Mary. As for Martin Hayle — he was as handsome as a Greek god, and had just got all sorts of honours at Oxford and was a rowing-blue; naturally *he* wouldn't look at her while Carol was there, or any of the other pretty Dene Park girls.

'Poor old Mary,' said Judy to herself;

'she's got the jitters to-night.'

Then she danced downstairs to the drawing-room to greet the first guests of the party who were just arriving.

Mary was forgotten.

Of course Mary was late for dinner. Everybody had started by the time she entered the dining-room which she had slaved all day to decorate and which looked so gay with its scarlet and silver paper bells dangling across the ceiling, its one huge silver bell full of crackers just over the centre of the table. And naturally when Mary entered the room she became the cynosure of all eyes. But the party did not stare at her because she was pretty and good to look at, which she well knew. She was painfully nervous and sensitive and walked awkwardly to her chair and sat down, lashes lowered, cheeks hot.

She was only too miserably aware that she looked a sight. She had cried violently after Judy's cruel remark about Mr. Cortright, and her eyelids were red, her nose pink and shiny in spite of its coat of powder. Even the new frock did not suit her.

'Poor old Mary,' thought Carol, who was radiant and conscious of her charms, seated next to the man she favoured.

'How unattractive she is,' was the reflection of that particular man, Martin Hayle, as he looked at Carol's sister.

Once Mary looked straight across the table over a crystal vase of red Christmas roses, at the man for whom she had always cherished a forlorn love. Martin Hayle, fresh from victories and honours at the 'Varsity, was certainly good to look at: six-foot-two; broad shoulders, smooth dark head, bright hazel eyes set in a handsome sun-bronzed face. He was just twenty-four and about to enter his father's office in the City. Mr. Hayle was a stockbroker of moderate means and Martin was the only son. He was a trifle spoiled, a little elated by youthful successes, with the knowledge that all the world lay before him. But he was a charming personality and full of kindness.

He had known the Everests for years and it was second nature to him to flirt with pretty Carol, although he had no intention of marrying her or any woman at the moment. It was also second nature to him to overlook Mary. She was a nice, kind, sweet-tempered girl, always ready to do a fellow a good turn; but she could not dance with him or look pretty or do any of the things Martin liked a boon companion to do.

While the Christmas toasts were being drunk he suddenly became aware that Mary's dark, rather sullen eyes were fixed upon him and that she was drinking her toast especially to him. It gave him a slight shock. He stared at the slender girl in the severe black velvet gown, at the brown hair twisted into that old-fashioned bun, the pale, rather pathetic face.

'Poor little thing,' he thought kindly. He raised his glass toward her and smiled. 'Merry Christmas, Mary!' he said.

That smile (Martin had a very winning smile) and those few words sent the blood flying to her cheeks. Her heart thrilled.

'Thank you,' she whispered.

But he had not waited to hear the thanks. He had bent his dark handsome head to the golden one of Carol and was whispering some merry word that was making her laugh at him.

Mary's flush faded. She set down her glass. The guests trooped into the drawing-room. She found herself quite alone, staring at the disordered table with its pile of torn crackers and empty nutshells and drained glasses. She felt piteously lonely. Slowly she walked past the mirror, caught sight of her thin pale face and bit so savagely at her lip that it bled.

'Oh, God, God! Why didn't You make me beautiful?' cried her aching, hungry heart.

The B.B.C. Dance Band filled the big lounge with gay music. Couples were dancing. Mary saw Martin steering Carol round the room. She looked radiant in the circle of that strong arm.

Mary looked down at the floor, remembered dully how her back had ached helping Alice to beeswax and polish it for the dance. But she did not participate in the pleasures it afforded. Not a young man in the room thought of asking Mary Everest to dance. They were all busy with their young, gay, pretty partners.

She felt somehow that it was the worst Christmas Eve she had ever spent. Perhaps because she had grown to care for Martin Hayle so much since last December. And what use to care? He ignored her, probably laughed at her in his heart, was kind because he was sorry for her. That was a humiliating thought.

Mary stared forlornly at the new wrist-watch her father had given her. It was a pretty, expensive thing; but she would rather have had one word of praise about her hair, or her frock, or her appearance in general. That would have thrilled and comforted her, been the loveliest present she could have received. A wrist-watch was cold comfort.

As the night wore on the fun waxed fast and furious. There was a good deal of laughing and kissing under the mistletoe. Mary had hung it up. But nobody kissed Mary. She stood by and with hard, tearless eyes saw Martin catch several girls in his arms and give them a kiss for which she would have forfeited half her possessions — nay, the whole!

Midnight came. Mary felt deathly tired and sick of the festivities around her. She had talked to old Cortright, sat with her father, exchanged a few words with one or two women friends. Now, heavy-eyed and bored she wished for bed, for sleep and forgetfulness. Sometimes in her dreams she was beautiful . . . she was being courted by Martin Hayle. She had nothing but her dreams!

Unconsciously she had placed herself, in this moment, under a bunch of mistletoe. Martin Hayle had just finished a tango with Sheila Martin. Sheila saw Mary's lonely little figure and whispered to Martin:

'There's Mary Everest standing under the mistletoe. Does she think she might get kissed? Poor Mary — isn't it funny she should be so plain with Carol and

11

Judy her sisters? I can't *think* why she wears such long skirts and has that awful bun of hair!'

Martin's bright hazel eyes rested on the forlorn figure a second. Then suddenly he left Sheila's side, marched up to Mary, put an arm round her shoulder and kissed her lightly on the mouth.

Most of the people in the room saw the incident and a ripple of laughter went round. Mary, to whom the caress had been a shock and an exquisite pleasure and pain combined, stood motionless, cheeks scarlet, one hand up to the lips he had kissed.

'Oh . . . !' she whispered. 'Oh . . . !'

She felt that the very earth stood still . . . that she was suddenly a goddess . . . because Martin's lips had touched hers . . . because for one thrilling, unforgettable instant she had felt his arm about her.

And for a moment her plain face was transfigured by acute happiness, her brown eyes were like stars.

But five minutes later she was dashed

from the heights of bliss to the depths of a greater despair than she had ever known in her life. On her way up to her room she came across Martin and Carol sitting out in the hall, their backs turned to her. And Carol was saying in her cool, cruel voice:

'Everyone was *frightfully* amused to see you kiss Mary under the mistletoe. It was *kind* of you, Martin!'

'Oh, not at all,' came his reply. 'But the poor girl looked so forlorn, I felt sorry for her. I assure you I didn't want to kiss her.'

Mary's heart sank. Every vestige of colour left her cheeks. The bitterness, the humiliation of her thoughts became intolerable. So he had not wanted to kiss her ... he had just been sorry for her ... and the others had been '*frightfully amused*.'

Mary rushed up to her bedroom, flung herself on her bed and lay there, shivering, biting her handkerchief to keep herself from screaming aloud.

'Oh, God, oh, God, I hate them — I

hate them all!' she moaned, her fingers clawing the pillow. 'Oh, if I could pay them back . . . make them suffer as I suffer!'

To-night's experience turned the naturally sweet, sympathetic girl into a bitter, infuriated, insulted woman. She was denied her rightful heritage of fun, love, of laughter. She was pitied, sneered at, neglected. And Martin . . . Martin for whom she would have died, had made a laughing stock of her out of careless pity.

She felt raw . . . as though something inside her heart was bleeding, crushing, killing her. If only she could pay them back . . . if she could by a miracle become beautiful, outshine all those self-satisfied women downstairs, leave those sisters of hers in the background, make men like Martin Hayle and Chris Miller break their hearts for her!

But it was hopeless — useless, all this agony of shame and misery, this tormenting hunger for admiration and love. One thing she decided this Christmas Eve . . . one definite resolve formed in her half-crazed brain. She would run away from home — leave Dene Park and The Grange — to go where she would be unknown and where her family would never find her.

She had saved up fifty or sixty pounds of her allowance. She bought so little, was never extravagant. She would take that money from the locked cash-box in her trunk and go away early to-morrow — Christmas morning. She would leave a note for her father telling him she could not bear life at home any more and that she was going abroad to find some sort of work. She could speak French quite well. Yes, she might go to Paris — get into a French family as a governess — anything, anything rather than stay in Dene Park and be the object of derision and pity to the people who knew her and her family.

Mary was a strong-minded girl. Having once made such a decision she would keep it. In the early hours of the morning, with the sounds of music and revelry floating up the stairs to her, she packed a suitcase and made her plans. Last thing before going to bed she stood before her dressing-table, white, shivering with passionate emotion, tight-lipped, eyes red and swollen with weeping. In her fingers she held a snapshot of Martin which she had taken last summer . . . Martin in white flannels on the tennis-court here, at The Grange. He was smiling at the photographer . . . handsome head thrown back, racquet in his hands.

Mary stared at the pictured face, the most bitter pain and desolation in her heart.

'No wonder you didn't want to kiss me,' she said aloud. 'A plain, wretched, hopeless girl like me . . . but oh, Martin. my dear, my darling. I'd have given my life for you if you'd needed it.'

Then her mood changed. She tore the snapshot in half.

'You've been cruel — you've derided me with the rest,' she muttered. 'Even your kiss was an insult. I hate you like I hate them all.'

⋆ ⋆ ⋆

On Christmas morning when the rest of the Everest family lay soundly sleeping, Mary left home.

At midday she was on the Channel crossing over to Calais. She had no difficulty in getting her ticket and was already in possession of a passport, having travelled to Paris with her father on business, twelve months ago. It was a rough crossing this Christmas morning — a raw, bitterly cold day. The sea was choppy, and as the boat neared France, it headed straight into a grey fog, but Mary did not care. She was like a dead thing. Mute, white, indifferent to fate, she had but one passionate wish like a live coal smouldering in the ashes of despair . . . that she might get right away from everybody who had ever known or pitied her.

She felt no regret that she had left home. Dad might fret a bit, but would soon get over it. Carol was his darling. Carol and Judy and Jack would not care — only say 'Poor old Mary,' or 'a bit off her nut,' or 'sort of silly thing one might expect her to do' . . . etc., etc.

Her lips curled at the thought of the family comments at breakfast. At least they would not be nervous about her. She was not pretty enough to cause anxiety about her being stolen or led away by men!

She had decided to go to Paris. Raw, chilled, apathetic, she took her seat in the Calais-Paris express.

There was still a thick fog over land and sea, and just outside the town of Amiens the train crashed into another express, which was coming through from Bale to Boulogne. It was a frightful collision, resulting in the telescoping and wrecking of many coaches and a heavy list of 'killed and injured.'

Mary Everest remembered nothing beyond the sudden sickening crash and shock of a collision . . . of flying splintered wood and glass . . . then of agonising pain in her face and head. She was thrown forward onto the floor. After that came darkness and silence.

Later still she went through a strange period of what seemed a nightmare, but was semi-consciousness and at times complete oblivion. She dimly heard hoarse cries and a sharp scream for help . . . felt herself being lifted into somebody's arms . . . heard her own voice as from a great distance, moaning, moaning . . .

Once she woke right up to pain so frightful that she shrieked aloud and flung her hands up to her cheeks. Then a mask was put over her face and she breathed in a sweet, sickly scent of ether and chloroform, and after that she lost consciousness again.

It seemed to her years and years before she returned to real sensibility. In reality she went through many days in a drugged stupor, occasionally conscious of pain, crying out, then feeling the prick of a hypodermic needle in her arm, or a gentle, soothing touch of her hand. Sometimes she dozed or slept naturally, sometimes heard voices both of men and women, but never quite realised where she was or what was happening to her. It was one long bad dream to Mary. She suffered quite a lot in spite of the morphia which drugged her poor, racked body and brain. But she was too weak and stupefied to complain much or worry as to where she was or what had become of her.

Then one morning — it must have been while her face was being dressed — she became more normal and alive to sound and touch. She groaned and tried to move, opened heavy eyes and saw a man in a white coat and two nurses in uniform by her side. She also saw that she was in a narrow white bed surrounded by screens.

'Oh!' she said. 'Oh . . .'

'Don't move, ma'mselle,' said the man, in French, deftly putting a mask of wool over her face, with slits for eyes, nose and mouth. 'Just one minute, please.'

Mary submitted wearily to one of the nurses who bandaged her face and head with swift, skilled fingers. Then she said in a weak, hoarse little voice:

'Where am I? What has happened to me?'

The nurse smiled at her and shrugged her shoulders, intimating that she was French and could not understand English. The man moved to her side again and sat down by her. The nurses quietly retired behind the screens.

'Tell me — ' whispered Mary.

'You are English, ma'mselle?' said the man in her own tongue, carefully correctly spoken.

'Yes.'

'When you were brought in from the train we looked for a card or letter to identify you but found none,' he continued. 'Your name is — ?'

'Mary Everest.'

'Your address?'

'That — doesn't matter,' said Mary slowly.

'You do not wish us to notify your relations or friends?'

'N-o,' she replied. 'It doesn't matter.'

'Very well,' he said. 'You remember

you were in the Paris express which was wrecked at Amiens. This is a hospital in Amiens. You have been here two weeks.'

'Two weeks!' she whispered, amazed. 'Then it is January!'

'Yes, the New Year is past.'

Sudden pain throbbed in her bandaged face and head. She groaned. At once he bent over her.

'I am Dr. Rhodes,' he said. 'I am Greek — not French, and am taking a special interest in your case. Don't worry — just leave yourself in my hands.'

Mary closed her eyes and went on moaning. She had already lost interest in everything except her pain — terrible pain that throbbed through her ears, her very brain.

Then came the prick of the hypodermic needle . . . within half an hour, blessed relief, the stupor of drugged sleep.

The next morning, however, she awoke to clearer consciousness and a greater interest in things. She asked Dr. Rhodes (who was one of the few in the hospital who spoke English fluently) many questions. She learned that she had narrowly escaped death; that two of the unfortunate people in her carriage had met their ends in that frightful collision. But when she was told that it was her face and head which had suffered and not her body, she gave a bitter, mirthless little laugh that perplexed the nurses.

'My face! It would be my face . . . it is my face that has caused all the tragedy in my life,' she muttered.

Then she begged for a mirror.

'Let me see the worst,' she said hysterically. 'Let me see what I'm like — a gargoyle now, instead of just a plain girl, I suppose. But I don't care . . . I only wish I'd died! Give me a mirror.'

She was gently but firmly refused the glass. The French nurses, kind, sympathetic, but at a loss with the patient whose language they did not understand, tried to soothe her in vain. Finally the doctor in charge of her case was sent for. She was so restless and hysterical that her temperature was mounting.

'*Le bon docteur* Rhodes is wonderful

— he is great, the greatest plastic surgeon alive, he has performed miraculous facial operations,' one of the nurses stammered in broken English. '*Restez tranquille, ma'mselle.*'

But Mary moaned and tossed until Rhodes came and sat at her side. Then he took one of her hands in a grasp which was particularly strong and soothing.

'Hush,' he said. 'If you work up to this state you will do your face infinite harm.'

'I don't care — I was ugly before — now I must be hideous,' she said, great tears forcing their way through the slits in the swathing of bandages.

'Hush,' he said again. 'Forget everything — only leave yourself in my hands and try to get well. Hush, I command that you compose yourself.'

His voice was very deep and rich, with a note of strange power and authority. Mary ceased crying and lay still, staring up at him. For the first time she looked at him as a person, not as a white-coated machine who alternately hurt and helped her. She became suddenly aware of his curiously strong, compelling personality as well as his physical good looks. He was a very big man, with a massive head that was pure Greek, and covered with dark red curls.

The face was handsome, marble-pale, with clever light grey eyes. A powerful, fascinating face . . . although strangely sinister, because of its queer hardness and coldness and the thin, cruel mouth. Just for a moment Mary was interested in him. Then she lapsed back into apathy, misery, indifference as to her fate. But he had quietened her, and letting go her hand, noiselessly left her bedside.

The days slipped by — one very much like another. Mary grew accustomed to the sights and sounds of a French hospital ward, and to the ever-powerful and compelling personality of the Greek surgeon. Sometimes other doctors came; students, nurses, grouped about her bed. Rhodes lectured to them in French much too difficult for her to understand, but obviously about her face. It did not anger or interest her. She was indifferent to everything but the occasional pain she suffered.

One day Rhodes told her that she was going to be moved from the hospital.

'With your permission I am taking you in an ambulance to my own private nursing-home, attached to my house on the outskirts of Amiens,' he said. 'There you will undergo one more operation, but it will not cause you much pain, I promise, and my nurses are the finest in the world. My sister, Irene Rhodes, who lives with me, keeps house for me, will also take the greatest interest in your case.'

'I don't care what happens to me,' said Mary. 'But why take all this trouble? Why not let me die?'

A peculiar smile curved his thin lips.

'Basil Rhodes has never let any patient die yet who could possibly be saved,' he said. 'And in you I am especially interested.'

'Why?'

He did not answer.

On the following day Mary was removed to Rhodes' private home. She saw nothing of the journey, nor the big, fine grounds surrounding the old French château which Rhodes had bought and turned into a veritable palace of luxury. He and his sister occupied the château with a retinue of servants. The Greeks were immensely wealthy. Attached to the place was a small house which the doctor had built containing two or three bedrooms, a wonderful surgery with all the latest electrical appliances, a special room for X-rays and a laboratory. Two trained nurses and a medical assistant, a clever young Frenchman, worked there.

Mary knew nothing of this, nor of the way the place was run, nor of the immense amount of money spent on her. It only seemed to her that it was a waste of time — of the Greek doctor's time — to bring her here. She fully intended to throw herself into the river when she was allowed to go free and to look at her disfigured face.

She was indifferent even to the luxury of her new quarters; a bedroom to herself — a magnificent room overlooking the spacious grounds of the château, and full of beautiful flowers, presumably from the hot-houses attached to the place.

The second operation was performed in Rhodes' own little theatre. The Frenchman, Lefevre by name, gave the anaesthetic. It was over quickly and when Mary opened her eyes she felt sick and miserable but suffered very little pain. She heard Rhodes talking — apparently to his assistant. He spoke in rapid French, but Mary knew enough of the language to comprehend some of the conversation.

'It is wonderful, is it not, Lefevre?' he said.

'A miracle! You are a genius, sir,' was Lefevre's reply.

A miracle! What was a miracle? Mary wondered. She moved her bandaged head wearily and wished they would leave her alone and let her find complete oblivion in death.

After that operation she grew rapidly stronger and the bandages were removed from her face, the air was allowed to get at her skin and head again. Her hair had been cut off — she could feel that. But she was not yet allowed the mirror which she began to demand incessantly again. She supposed she was so hideous that they were loath to let her see herself and felt sick at the thought. Once or twice Irene Rhodes, the surgeon's sister, came to see her. Mary did not like the Greek woman. She was a tall, statuesque creature with her brother's red hair and marble-pale face, but she was cold and stiff with Mary, only spoke a few words, then departed. The only thing Mary felt grateful to her for was that no expression of any kind changed her face when she first looked down at Mary, who already dreaded strangers, and dreaded to see a look of repulsion or distaste.

Miss Rhodes merely glanced at her, then said something in Greek to her brother. The doctor was not expressionless, however. He was rather flushed and excited, and his light grey eyes glittered at he looked at his patient. He nodded and answered his sister in a voice that sounded triumphant.

Mary wondered what he said and why he was pleased.

She had grown used to the sight of him, to the dominant personality of the man. Every day for an hour he sat with her, talking of everything under the sun except herself. He lent her many clever books, interested her by helping her to improve her slight knowledge of French so that she could converse more freely with Lefevre and the nurses. And sometimes doctors from outside came in and looked at her, jotted down notes, appeared to be praising and congratulating Rhodes.

She grew restive and sick of the mystery surrounding her appearance.

'Give me a mirror — let me know the worst,' she begged him one morning.

'Next week,' he said in a quiet voice. 'I promise you shall have a mirror next week. It is now over seven months.'

She was almost shocked.

'Seven months! And it is summer-time. It was Christmas Day when I left home.

Now it is warm . . . July!'

'Yes,' he said. 'And you still have no desire to send for a relative or friend?'

'No,' she said harshly. 'I am dead to them. And I only wish I had died. Life was insupportable before, when I was just plain . . . now I can't bear the thought of commencing afresh with this disfigurement.'

He gave a queer smile and took her hand in his.

'Courage,' he said. 'Wait until — next week.'

After he had gone she sobbed weakly to herself. Seven months had passed. The summer sun streamed into her beautiful bedroom and she was being taken care of with infinite trouble and surrounded by luxuries. Yet she wished she had died on Christmas Day . . . failed to understand why all these queer doctors and nurses beamed at her, gesticulated and smiled and seemed so pleased about everything.

She was now allowed to sit up in an armchair and be dressed. That next week she grew much stronger, walked about

31

and took a shade more interest in the château and garden. On the Sunday the day nurse in charge of her case put her into a new frock which Irene Rhodes had bought and sent to her. It was a graceful little gown of pale grey silken material, with delicate Puritan collar and cuffs of ivory georgette — very French — very expensive. Mary looked at it with bitterness.

'It's beautiful, but of little use to a girl having a hideous face,' she said to the nurse. The woman smiled — a secret, satisfied little smile that annoyed Mary.

'Wait till the *bon docteur* comes, ma'mselle,' she murmured.

Basil Rhodes entered her room that morning carrying a large Queen Anne looking-glass which he placed on the dressing-table. Then he came up to Mary who was standing by the window, gloomily surveying the riot of flowers in the sunny garden.

'Now,' he said, his voice throbbing in a strange way. 'Now — you may see — your face!'

She stared up at him, then began to shudder.

'I can't — I'm afraid to — *now*!'

'Come,' he said in a masterful way. 'Come ...'

He drew her towards the mirror, strong, ruthless fingers gripping hers, and when she reached it he released her.

'Look, Mary Everest,' he said in a voice of extreme exultation. 'Look and tell me if you recognise yourself.'

She looked ... she stared ... for the first time for seven long months she saw herself in a glass. For what seemed an eternity, she stared and stared with great brown eyes that looked back at her, amazed, incredulous.

She did not recognise herself.

It was a new girl there before her. Of the original Mary only the graceful figure and rich brown head remained, and the dark eyes that had always been beautiful, thickly lashed. But even her figure had changed. Months of good food, of rest, of comparative peace had taken away the hollows on throat and cheeks.

She was no longer too thin.

But the face was a miracle. Unbelieving she stared at it as though at an apparition. It was the same oval shape, but the cheeks had filled out, and the skin was like that of a newborn babe, pink, smooth, exquisitely soft with the blush of perfect health. The mouth that Dr. Rhodes had moulded to his liking, out of what had been a mangled misshapen mass, was full, scarlet, curved. The nose was straight, finely chiselled. The forehead smooth and white. The rich brown hair was glossily brushed into crisp short curls.

It was the face of a beautiful woman ... dangerously beautiful, because it still had character. It was not merely a mask. It was a face with charm — alluring and full of strange fascination.

Mary stared long and hard until her cheeks became brilliant red and her breath came in short gasps. Then she put her fingers up to her face.

'My God, it can't be true!' she stuttered.

'It is true,' said Basil Rhodes behind her. 'Are you pleased, Mary Everest?'

She swung round to him.

'You have done this — this miracle — made me so beautiful?' she gasped.

He took her arms and stared down at her. He was so close she could feel his great body trembling, and there was a gleam of an almost fanatical worship in his eyes.

'Yes, I have done it. I am your creator,' he said in a deep booming voice. 'Now, do you wish to die — do you hate me for letting you live?'

She broke loose from him, once more turned and stared at her reflection, stared with dilated dark eyes at her new face. Great sobs convulsed her slender body — sobs of wild excitement, of rapturous amazement.

'I can't believe it yet . . . if, is that me . . . that beautiful girl — with such a skin . . . such a mouth . . .'

'Such a mouth,' echoed the doctor, under his breath, 'ah, that is exquisite, like the mouth of Psyche, passionate and alluring . . .'

'How have you done it?' she gasped. 'How did you do it — tell me!'

'All my life I have wanted to perform such a miracle,' he said. 'I have studied plastic surgery — worked, practised, re-moulded, experimented until I reached perfection. During the war I made handsome men of seamed wrecks . . . once before you I made an ugly woman passable. But you are my supreme effort — my crowning triumph. For I have made you beautiful beyond dreams, remoulded what was a mangled, terrible face into the face of Psyche. Like an artist, a sculptor, I modelled you, worked on you, used all my power, my knowledge. And there is not a scar anywhere. You are perfect. Your nose, your mouth, your chin are lovely. Well-dressed you will be one of the most beautiful women in the world.'

She went on staring at herself while she listened to him. She was fascinated, entranced by her new face, like Narcissus, falling in love with the reflection of his own beauty. Then she turned back to the man who had created her, given her the marvellous gift of beauty for which she had always prayed, and gave him her hands.

'Thank you, thank you, thank you,' she said in a voice of hysterical joy. 'Oh how can I ever repay you? I was plain and unattractive and men passed me by, jeered at me. Now I am beautiful, and I owe it all to you!'

'Yes, to me,' he said. 'And I can give you more — the polish, the finish, of a woman of the world which should accompany such beauty — give you personality so that you will not be merely a lovely doll. I can take you to Paris, teach you to dance, to speak French, to wear beautiful clothes, turn you into a woman who shall dazzle Europe.'

She listened to him enthralled.

'But why? Why have you done so much and why do you offer to do more?' she said breathlessly. 'Oh, you are like a god to me, Dr. Rhodes — you have created me — I will do anything on earth to repay you.'

'Very well,' he said, flinging back his head. 'You shall marry me — repay me by becoming my wife. You are my creation. Do you understand what has happened? I have fallen in love with the beautiful woman I have made.'

She stared up at him, fascinated, yet a little frightened by the passion in his eyes and voice.

'You want to marry me?'

'Yes,' he said. 'I demand that as a return for what I have done for you.'

For a long while she did not speak. The first flush of excitement, of rapture at her new-gained beauty had died down.

She was a new being . . . yet the same Mary Everest inside. And the old bitter, cynical thoughts were still there, the old desire to revenge herself on those who had sneered and jeered at her returned in full force.

If she could go back to Dene Park, go back to The Grange — ride triumphantly over Carol, Judy, Sheila Martin — put them in the shade with her new, wondrous beauty . . . ah, that would be triumph indeed! If she could see the glow of admiration in the eyes of Martin Hayle . . . of the men who had neglected her, passed her by, laughed at Martin for kissing her on Christmas Eve . . . what an intoxicating thought!

The idea of bringing Martin to her feet particularly thrilled her. She felt strangely hard and vengeful. She wanted to break his heart . . . she was already consumed with a new passion . . . a passion to break the hearts of all the men she met . . . make them her playthings. So long she had been ugly, neglected, hungry for love. Now she was beautiful and could get what she wanted. She was infinitely more lovely than Carol or any woman in Dene Park. She could laugh at them all.

She was too intoxicated with her new power to realise the gravity of what she did or said . . . to sense the evil in this Greek surgeon who wanted to possess her body and soul.

So she lifted the hands that had made

her beautiful and kissed them.

'I will marry you,' she said feverishly. 'I will marry you on one condition.'

He swept her into his arms and held her against him.

'What?' he said. 'I will give you anything within reason, you desirable creature!'

'One year of freedom,' she pleaded. 'One year to go back to England to my old home. You have never asked me any questions and I know you are too great-minded to ask them now, to worry over any trifling revenge or triumph I may desire. But just give me one year of freedom — let me do what I want — then at the end of it — I will come back to you.'

He hesitated, his strange eyes narrowed.

'A whole year ... it is very long ... when I want you ... Basil Rhodes, who has never wanted a woman before.'

'Six months of it I will spend with you in Paris,' Mary said breathlessly. 'You shall teach me to dance, to talk, to gain the necessary polish and finish ... then six months in England, and then I will come back.'

'Very well,' he said, flinging back his arrogant head. 'Why not? It is a fair bargain. You shall go back and I shall ask no questions. I shall re-christen you 'Viva' which means life. Mrs. Viva Rhodes, a Greek heiress, and the fairest woman in Greece, you shall return to them who knew you as Mary Everest.'

Mary . . . henceforth to be known as Viva Rhodes . . . turned her head to the mirror, laughed at her own lovely laughing face in the glass.

She was crazy with excitement, with the prospect of being able to avenge that poor, miserable, plain girl who had run away from The Grange.

'Viva,' said the Greek, his lips close to her ear, 'you are mine, you belong to me, beloved. But I will ask nothing of you until you return to marry me, except one kiss . . . one kiss to seal our compact.'

She looked up at him, shivering a little. She did not love him, did not want

41

to marry him. But she was immensely grateful to him for the beauty he had given her, grateful to the pitch of intoxication. She surrendered herself to his kiss — the first kiss of passion any man had laid on the lips of the old Mary or of the new Viva.

2

When Irene Rhodes knew that her brother meant to marry the girl he had turned into a creature of loveliness, her jealousy and anger were limitless. But she was too clever to let Basil or Viva see what she felt. She was controlled but deadly cold and venomous. Wait until the girl was sent back to England. She would set to work then to woo her brother from any idea of future marriage with this Viva who had no right to the name of Rhodes now or ever.

Meanwhile Irene obeyed her brother. She accompanied him and Viva to Paris. There the girl was fitted out with a gorgeous trouseau: taught by the finest master in that city of pleasure to dance; given every chance to acquire the polish, the finish of the woman of the world.

Her new beauty gave her courage and roused in her the most passionate desire to learn, to achieve, to ride over the heads of the other women she saw around her. There was nothing in her way, and the immense wealth of the Rhodes to assist her. They stayed in Paris until November. And all the while the Greek quietly assisted in the education of his pupil and satisfied himself at the finish that she was perfect — ready for victory.

She had always been graceful — awkward only because so shy. Now she danced with exquisite finish — Carol or Judy would have looked gawky beside her. She had learned to dress with all the taste and artistry of a Frenchwoman. She could smoke, drive a car, do all that she had once found impossible. She was in fact, a perfect product of the post-war era. To use her eyes effectively, to flirt a little, came naturally to her now, just as it comes to all very pretty women. She had tasted the sweets of admiration at last ... had grown intoxicated by triumph when, at her first public dinner in Paris, men turned to look at her, continued to look ... and women, too, stared and envied her.

The shy, plain, unhappy Mary Everest was a beautiful, fascinating woman of the world. To have once been ugly and ignored and to become what she was now was indiscribable bliss. It was pure joy to see her steal a glance at her own reflection in a mirror as she passed through a hotel lounge with the Rhodes, or dressed in her bedroom for a dance. She was a slim, enchanting creature who wore smart clothes and who had an adorable brown head; great dark eyes; and pale skin; lips touched to deep sweet rose.

But under the beauty and triumph the bitterness against her family and their friends remained. She grew hard and vindictive at the memory of them. She felt the most passionate longing for the hour when she could go back . . . conquer . . . be avenged!

The time came.

It was Christmas again . . . approaching Christmas Eve. Basil Rhodes did not want to let her go — the beautiful Viva of his creation, who had become the passionate desire of his life.

But he had promised her that year of freedom and kept his word.

He saw her off from Boulogne on Christmas Eve.

'You have arranged everything?' he said, as he stood by her waiting for her to depart.

'Everything,' she said. 'Two days ago I sent a letter, which your sister wrote so that my handwriting should not be recognised, to my sister Carol. I said that I had met her sister Mary in Paris and become a friend of hers . . . that Mary had died of pneumonia and been buried there . . . that it was her wish that I should go to see her people. As Viva Rhodes I shall turn up at The Grange to-night. There will be a party in progress . . . the old customs are never ignored by the Everest family,' she added with a sneer in her voice. 'The old friends will be there, and Martin Hayle among them without doubt.'

'And you will burst upon them as a wonder of the age, you exquisite thing,' muttered Rhodes, staring down at her haughty, lovely little face. 'And you shall bring this fool Martin to your feet — then play with him. But remember at the promised time you come back to France — to me!'

She shivered and lowered her lashes. Then she laughed.

'Of course I owe everything to you. I shall not forget.'

'I have put a large sum of money to your credit in a bank in London,' he said. He handed her a paper. 'Here is the address. You will not want for cash and you can give out that you are heiress to a Greek relative.'

'They will open their mouths wide at Dene Park,' said Viva, 'just to imagine poor Mary could have made such a friend. The boat is going. Good-bye, and thank you.'

For a second Basil gripped her hands. His penetrating eyes burned down into hers.

'Remember,' he whispered. 'I made you Viva. You are forever mine.'

Those words haunted her long after

she had sailed away from France and from Dr. Rhodes' physical presence. She knew that she would never get really away from him . . . from his dominating, powerful mind.

But she tried to forget him. She put on dark glasses and sat comfortably in a deck-chair and smiled to herself as various men on the boat strolled by, glanced down at her, glanced again. It was wonderful to be admired. She felt she would never grow used to admiration — never blasée. It was the wine of life to her now.

Her thoughts were conflicting when, later that day, she found herself in a taxi driving from Victoria to Dene Park.

She took only a suitcase with her, had left her luggage at Victoria until she knew better what she intended to do. Everything depended on her family . . . on what they might say. All the better if they invited her to stay at The Grange. Then the fun would begin.

When first she leaned out of the car and saw the familiar outline of her old home, through the winter dusk, she felt a queer constriction of the throat — the sting of tears in her eyes. But that natural, affectionate feeling speedily passed. Dark, bitter thoughts of the misery, the loneliness she had endured there a year ago flooded her mind. She began to feel excited at the thought of her present beauty and power ... of the effect she would make this Christmas Eve.

Very, very different to the Christmas Eve of a year ago. She could hear music ... see the lights were on all over the house. Her heart beat so fast as she stepped out of the taxi, it seemed to suffocate her. Everything was the same ... just as she had pictured it. The customary Christmas Eve party was in progress.

She paid the taxi-driver and rang the front-door bell.

As she waited for the door to open she thought of Martin Hayle — wondered feverishly whether he would be there.

It so chanced that Martin was passing through the hall as the bell clanged. Dinner was not yet served. The maids were busy down in the kitchen. The Everests were in the drawing-room with their guests. Martin imagined he would do a kindness to the overworked maid if he opened the door. It was probably a late guest.

He was bored. Carol was pursuing him rather openly to-night and the whole atmosphere of the party had got on his nerves. His handsome face was a trifle sulky as he opened the front door.

Then he stood still and stared. He found himself looking at a stranger . . . the enchanting vision of a slim girl in a mink coat. He caught sight of a strangely beautiful face with large dark eyes. Then Viva stepped on to the threshold.

'May I come in?' she said. 'This is Mr. Everest's house, isn't it?'

'Yes,' said Martin, feeling suddenly unaccountably stirred. 'Do come in. I am Martin Hayle — a friend. May I ask your name?'

Just for the fraction of a second the new woman Viva Rhodes was seized with the desire to be the old humble, hungering Mary and to throw herself at his feet — to say, 'Look at me — I am beautiful — I am desirable — and I am your old friend Mary Everest — come home!'

But that desire was like a lightning flash — it passed. She gave him a slow smile.

'My name is Viva Rhodes,' she said, 'and I come with a message from Mr. Everest's daughter, Mary.'

Martin went on staring at her.

'I say, really? How extraordinary — but do come in, please — I'll tell Mr. Everest — he'll be delighted.'

The formal words, uttered with the typical courtesy of a man with a Public School and 'Varsity education, brought a slightly ironic curve to Viva's exquisite mouth. Delighted! That was scarcely the honest word. The family had never taken any interest in her during her lifetime at The Grange and would be merely curious about her now — not in the least delighted to receive news of her. With deepening irony Viva reflected that it was quite possible they might be relieved to hear of Mary's 'death.' It would be an ugly and unattractive member of the family off her father's hands!

Martin closed the door and led the unexpected guest to the drawing-room. Little did he know that she knew the way — was even more familiar with this house than he himself. He could not take his gaze from her — she fascinated him — whether by her unusual beauty or her personality, he could not tell.

Viva's heart pounded as he opened the door for her and she looked at the familiar drawing-room, full of familiar faces. She knew that not one of the family or friends would recognise her, yet she was in a state of extreme nervous excitement under her mask of chilly dignity.

She saw her father, a little stouter and balder, by the fireplace with his old friend, Mr. Cortright — the plain, elderly, typically care-worn City man whom Judy had so cruelly said would 'just suit Mary' last Christmas Eve. She saw Carol in the centre of a crowd — that was very familiar! — evidently relating some amusing story which was making the others laugh. One swift glance showed Viva the little difference in them all. Carol was as pretty as ever, although a trifle too plump, and her golden hair was badly cut. It was rather untidy, straight with short wisps. She had a new, pretty frock for the Noel festivities — a pink and silver brocade which the old Mary would have thought smart and bitterly envied, but at which Viva Rhodes, with her trunks full of costly Dior dresses, furs, hats, jewels from the Rue de la Paix, smiled dryly and thought how provincial it looked. There was Judy, curly red hair shorter than ever, and Viva thought she had grown half an inch taller and was a trifle too thin with it; there was Chris Miller, rather better-looking than the Chris of a year ago — he had filled out — was more manly. Viva's brilliant eyes sped from face to face . . . all recognisable; Martin's sister, Betty, or Mrs. Page-Roper; Sheila Martin. It amused Viva to remember that Sheila was one of the 'beauties' of Dene Park. With her new knowledge of beauty and culture it struck her that Sheila was nondescript — would never be noticed in the lounge of a big hotel in Paris.

Martin Hayle called Carol Everest.

'Carol — this is Miss — er — Rhodes. I happened to open the door to her — she — she's a friend of Mary's.'

Carol ceased chatting and laughing and stared at the stranger in the mink coat. Everybody stopped talking and stared. Complete silence fell, and universal attention became centred on Viva. It was exactly what she wanted. She had meant to make an impression, to burst upon them like a bombshell this Christmas Eve.

Then Carol moved forward slowly.

'A friend of Mary's!' she exclaimed. 'You — you know our sister?'

'I knew her very well,' said Viva Rhodes in a low, husky voice . . . a cool, careful voice that fell on the ears of her hearers like running water. 'She sent me here to see you.'

The past tense was lost upon Carol for a moment. She became rather flurried. It had been her boast in days gone by to Mary that she was a 'perfect hostess' and never lost her head. But somehow under the curious penetrating gaze of the stranger's wonderful, brilliant dark eyes, she felt incredibly small and shy. Besides Carol was a true woman and in a glance had summed up Miss Rhodes' attire — guessed that the mink coat was worth thousands of pounds — that the small smart hat was the last word; that Mary's friend, whoever she was, looked most expensively dressed and had the air of a film star and the sort of face one saw on magazine covers or on the cinema screen.

'I — how exciting!' she said, flushed and flustered. 'I — do sit down — do take off your coat — we didn't expect you — where are you staying — oh, here's my father — '

She broke off in her stammered speech and indicated Mr. Everest who, after a surprised look through his glasses at the fair vision whose dramatic entrance had caused such a hush in the room, hurried forward.

'What's this?' he said. 'A friend of Mary's. Dear me, how surprising! I didn't catch your name — what is it? Rhodes, not an English name, surely!'

'No,' said Viva. 'I am half-Greek.'

'I'm not surprised,' muttered Chris in Judy's ear. 'She looks like a goddess. Have you ever seen such a girl?'

'She's certainly good-looking,' was Judy's very feminine and reluctant reply.

'Good-looking!' echoed Chris to himself. 'She's a glamour girl all right. Terrific.'

Viva found herself shaking hands with her father and greeting him as a stranger. It was queer, uncanny. Yet beyond the excitement, the triumph of it all, she did not care — did not feel any desire to throw herself on his neck and weep. She had never loved her father, nor had he loved her, except in a dutiful way. The sight of her sisters left her unmoved. She owed them too many a grudge; held too bitter memories of their neglect, their contemptuous treatment of her in the past.

The only human, soft emotion that seized her was at the sight of her young brother. He had never done anything for her, but he had never been definitely unkind. How he had grown, she thought with an affectionate glance at him. But his round blue eyes were staring blankly. Neither he nor anybody in that room doubted that the half-Greek, half-English stranger was Viva Rhodes. She did not in any way resemble poor Mary.

Viva found herself seated in a chair by the fire, being waited on by her flustered sisters. Carol had relieved her of her coat, Judy had taken her hat, Mr. Everest was questioning her about Mary.

She took her time before she answered the questions — turned to Martin Hayle, who from a distance was staring at her in that fascinated way.

'Have you a cigarette?' she asked coolly.

'Of course — here — ' he stammered. He lit it for her and she fixed it in a long holder. Mary Everest had never smoked, but Basil Rhodes had taught Viva the art and pleasure of it. Martin thought he had never seen anybody hold a cigarette more gracefully than this beautiful stranger, in her slim manicured fingers. And when he had bent down to light the cigarette he had caught a subtle stirring perfume from her ... he did not realise it, but it was a rare, expensive scent which Basil Rhodes had bought for her. The only one she ever used.

Just for an instant Viva looked up at him with a searching gaze. And now a pulse beat thickly in her throat as she remembered how she had worshipped this man and hungered and wept for him. He had changed very little physically; was as handsome as ever. But his manner was a little more poised and easy, and not so cheerful. She fancied he was worried or discontented with life.

Then she ignored him completely and began to talk to her family. They were all gathered about her, watching, questioning, listening. Carefully she told them the story she had prepared. She had met Mary Everest in Paris at the house of some women to whom she was governess ... had taken an instant fancy to her ... and later helped her when she grew ill and was practically starving in a room in Montmartre. But she had died of double-pneumonia and had asked that she, Miss Rhodes, should come to England and tell her family all about her.

The news of Mary's 'death' was received with mingled feeling and comments by the Everests. The atmosphere became naturally gloomy, and whatever the true feelings were, Carol and Judy and Jack and their father all expressed their grief to Miss Rhodes.

'Awful shock — never dreamed she was ill,' murmured Mr. Everest, with some genuine emotion.

'How awful — poor Mary!' chorused the girls.

'Rotten luck,' said Jack.

'Why didn't she send for one of us? She never wrote after she left — never let us help her,' added Carol (who although sorry was annoyed the news should have come and damped their spirits just in the middle of a Christmas party).

Viva drew a deep breath of her cigarette, then gave Carol a queer look from her dark slumberous eyes.

'Mary did not want any of you,' she said slowly.

'She always told me that none of you cared much about her because she was plain and unattractive, and pathetically observed just before she died that she would not be missed.'

Silence. Everybody looked uncomfortable and Carol and Judy exchanged quick glances which might almost be termed guilty. Mr. Everest, his feelings harrowed, broke into protests. The girls joined in. They all assured Miss Rhodes they had loved Mary, and never meant her to feel out of things . . . it was shocking to think she had died . . . what could they do to make up for it . . . and so on, while Viva listened, an ironic curve to her mouth. She knew how much of this talk was hypocritical; she knew how much better it would have been if these people had given the miserable, neglected Mary the love and attention they now wished to shower on her memory.

'How often it is the case . . . the dead receive the tears and sighs that might have made the days of the living so much happier,' she thought bitterly.

But it was not part of her scheme to allow her family to mourn or feel remorse — yet! They had despised her and driven her from their midst by their cruel indifference. She was going to get back at them. But later . . . in a much more subtle, certain way. She let them all babble of their sorrow and shocked feelings for a few moments . . . then let them pour out gratitude to her for being 'so kind to poor Mary' (ah! that 'poor' rankled even now in Viva's breast, so indicative it was of contemptuous pity); let them bless her for her goodness to their 'darling sister' and then, with a long look round at the flushed, dismayed faces about her, said, 'I must tell you this. Mary's last wishes — and very definite ones — were that none of you should wear mourning or make any difference — that you should be gay and happy just the same and forget her altogether.

'Well, well,' mumbled Mr. Everest. 'We ought to mourn decently — '

'No,' broke in Viva with a cold smile. 'She begged that you should not mourn at all, and in order to prevent you going to Paris to visit her grave she was cremated. She knew I would get here in time for Christmas and asked that I should take her place amongst you for the party.'

'It seems to me poor old Mary has been very decent,' Chris Miller whispered in Martin's ear.

Martin who had listened to Viva very intently, lit a cigarette and smoked it rather fiercely. His handsome eyes were moody.

'It makes me feel ashamed that none of us were more decent to her,' he muttered.

By the time Viva had finished with her family, told sufficient lies, spoken with sufficient eloquence, she had convinced them that they must not let Mary's 'death' upset them, but go on with life as though she had never existed. She had planted the first seeds of guilt in their hearts. That was enough for the moment. Then she changed her solemn manner to one of extreme gaiety and wit and a brilliant charm that completely enslaved them all; set them laughing, thrilled them with her enchantment.

'Of course you must stay with us — Carol, show Miss Rhodes to the guest-room,' said Mr. Everest. 'She has been so good to Mary — she must indeed take her place this Christmas, and since it was poor Mary's wish, we will go on with our party.' Carol, much relieved at this, hurried Viva to the guest-room. Judy followed, Chris Miller grabbed at the suitcase in the hall and sped after them. Those remaining in the drawing-room chattered amongst themselves and of course the conversation was entirely of Viva Rhodes.

'How fascinating . . .'

'Extremely beautiful . . .'

'Must have been good to Mary ... Fancy a stodgy, plain girl like Mary picking up such a friend ... '

'What clothes ... my dear, must have cost a packet.'

These were just a few of the remarks about Viva.

And she had the immense satisfaction of dressing for dinner waited on hand and foot by the two sisters to whom she had once been 'Cinderella.' It was Carol who unpacked her suitcase. Judy who fetched hot water for her, because the maid was busy ... both of them who stood lost in admiration of the expensive, chic clothes, and of Miss Rhodes herself.

While she dressed, Viva questioned them — curious to know what had befallen her family and friends during this last year which had been a veritable eternity to her. And one of the first, most important things told her was of Carol's engagement.

'Possibly poor Mary told you that there was every chance of it,' Carol said with a little giggle, and a very self-satisfied look in her large blue eyes.

Viva looked at her intently.

'To whom are you engaged?' she asked.

But she knew the answer before it was given. Her heart gave a swift throb.

'Martin Hayle,' said Carol. 'The young man who opened the door to you.'

Silence. Then Viva's beautiful mouth curved into a slow, secretive smile, although her dark eyes glittered.

She was standing before the wardrobe mirror now, regarding her reflection. She was ready to join the festive throng downstairs.

'How do I look?' she said sweetly, and glanced at each of her sisters in turn. They stared at her with bated breath.

'Oh — you look wonderful!' they chorused.

Viva flung back her head with a proud little gesture.

There she stood, radiant, in a ballet-length dress of grey Chantilly lace with dark red roses at her waist and her bare shoulders caressed by an exquisite stole of mutation mink. Carol and Judy looked dowdy, washed-out, heavy and dull, like candle-lights dimmed by the brilliant flash of an electric light in comparison.

The triumphant, vengeful thought leaped to Viva's mind.

'Martin's engagement to Carol will not last very long!'

There was plenty more for Viva to learn about her relations and friends that eventful night. By tactful questioning, careful that she never gave away her intimate knowledge of the family, she learned of the several changes that had taken place.

Martin Hayle was on the Stock Exchange with his father now. Carol expressed the lingering hope that he would marry her this coming spring. Chris Miller was on the point of becoming Judy's fiancé, but Mr. Everest considered Judy too young and wanted her to wait for her nineteenth birthday. Jack had left school and was with his father in the wholesale wine and spirit business. Sheila Martin was Miss Martin no longer. She had married Tom Sharron last July and they occupied a small house in Dene Park.

Viva smiled to herself as she looked at Sheila's pleased, smug little face and her husband's equally smug one.

'Poor fools,' she thought. 'If they only knew how dull, how unattractive they seem to me.'

Only one person in the room retained any of his former attraction. That was Martin Hayle — Martin, the most polished, brilliant, good-looking of that crowd. But he was Carol's fiancé; had placed that beautiful ring (of Carol's choosing) on her finger not long ago in a weak moment, imagining himself in love. But Viva Rhodes, watching, watching . . . the whole evening . . . knew that he was not in love with Carol. Carol pursued him, clung to his arm, treated him with an air of possession. But although he smiled at her, was even affectionate, it seemed to Viva that his manner was tired and bored.

'Wait,' she reflected grimly. 'Wait, Martin . . . my turn will come and then — you will wake up too late!'

But she was too clever to pay any particular attention to him that night. If anything she ignored him, which roused his curiosity. He thought he had never seen a more enchanting vision than she made. He had to force himself to remain glued to Carol's side; to try and find her plump pink-and-white prettiness attractive. But it was to Viva's beautiful, inscrutable face that his gaze constantly turned. She was the life and soul of the party — had invested it with a new thrill, an unusual brilliance — for Dene Park.

At the dinner table she sat on Mr. Everest's right hand. Martin was next to her, Chris Miller and Judy opposite. There, Martin could catch that elusive, fascinating perfume from her, found himself forgetting to talk to Carol, listening to the witty, amusing talk that flowed so easily from the lips of the girl who had been poor Mary Everest's 'great friend.'

But Viva, although subtly conscious of his proximity, his scrutiny, was focussing her attention upon Chris Miller just now. Chris had been asked to dance with her last Christmas Eve and had sniggered and grimaced. She would never, never forget that. She looked through half-closed eyes at his nice, tanned, boyish face and rather stupid blue eyes, and mentally laughed at him. The fool! The conceited young fool.

He would pay, bitterly for that grimace and refusal of a year ago. Already he was in her coils — unable to tear his gaze from her — stared open-mouthed across the flower-decked, candle-lit table at her and evidently found her a veritable magnet. He completely ignored Judy. He suddenly noticed how thin, how gawky, how silly she was. He went on staring at the goddess opposite him, and once she gave him the full benefit of her liquid dark eyes, felt his heart thud, his head grow dizzy.

The fun waxed hot and fast. Viva Rhodes had begged them not to let the news of 'Mary's death' damp their spirits and they willingly acceded to that request. During dessert toasts were drunk. Mr. Everest suggested the party should drink to Miss Rhodes, and Chris Miller, flushed with wine and excitement, his blue eyes gleaming down at the girl in her rose frock, leaped to his feet and seconded the toast.

'To our guest!' he said holding up his goblet.

Everybody drank. Viva sat motionless, chin cupped in her hand. But her lips smiled, and the taste of triumph was like honey in her mouth. She was the centre of attraction to-night. When crackers were pulled everybody wanted to pull one with her. Chris, reckless, intoxicated by her beauty and charm and the smiles she gave him, gave her all the stupid, sentimental mottoes he could find on the littered table, even handed her a toy ring and besought her to wear it. Inwardly she laughed! Ye gods, it was funny! And last Christmas Eve, Mary Everest had sat by Mr. Cortright, sullen and lonely and ignored, weeping tears of blood in her heart, tears of bitterness.

'Already you are being avenged, my Other Self,' Viva thought with a bitter smile.

But it was only the beginning. Viva Rhodes was insatiable in her desire for revenge.

Judy had insulted her by pairing her off with Mr. Cortright. To-night Judy sat neglected, sullen in her turn. She had begun to be jealous of Mary's marvellous friend. She did not like to see her Chris so flushed and excited about another woman. She tugged at his arm and whispered to him. He answered her impatiently and then went on talking to Viva.

After dinner she confided in her friend Sheila, now Mrs. Sharron, 'Do you like Miss Rhodes? I think she is a flirt. She is behaving very brazenly with Chris anyhow,' she said sulkily.

'H'm,' said Sheila, frowning, 'I'm not sure I trust her. My Tom keeps babbling about her. But of course she is stunning.'

'H'm,' said Judy in a reluctant way.

The usual dance to the radio was held in the drawing-room after dinner. Mary, a year ago, had sat alone neglected in a corner, miserably watching her sisters dance. To-night every man in the room hastened to beg for a dance. The first to secure a fox-trot was Chris — to-night the favoured one. He found her infinitely graceful, felt his foolish heart shake as he held her light, perfumed, adorable form in his arms. He danced with Judy afterwards and found her very different — hopping rather than dancing — clutching him. Of course Viva had been taught to dance by the finest master in Paris, and she was a Pavlova, in this room of second-rate dancers, to-night.

Then Martin, after his first duty-dance with Carol, asked Viva to waltz with him.

She was sitting by her father (how little he knew he was the father of this goddess!) smoking a cigarette, her wonderful eyes fixed broodingly on the crowd. When he spoke to her she looked up at him for a fraction of a moment.

'Not just now,' she said lazily. 'I'm rather tired, thanks very much.'

Martin flushed. The bored discontented look in his handsome grey eyes was replaced by one of resentment. Why should she refuse? She had danced with Tom, with Chris; why not with him? Did she think he would tread on her toes? He forgot that he was engaged to Carol and ought not to hanker after a dance with another woman. Viva's refusal had filled him with a stubborn wish to hold her in his arms.

'May I have the next then?'

She gave a little laugh and glanced at the jewelled watch on her delicate wrist.

'If I'm not in bed. I shan't stay up much later. I'm tired after my crossing to-day.'

'Please,' he said. 'Just one, Miss Rhodes.'

Ah! That satisfied her, thrilled her . . . to have this man pleading for a dance . . . this man who had kissed her 'out of pity' last Christmas Eve.

She kept him guessing, waiting; was

quite aware that he felt irritable because she ignored him, and that in consequence he was rather short with Carol who ran after him every minute. Then at last she graciously condescended to give him a tango. Carol knew the French tango — he knew it after a fashion and was a good dancer.

They found themselves alone on the floor, being eagerly watched by the others.

It was the most marvellous moment of Martin's life and the most intoxicating triumph for her. She knew he found her graceful, fairy-like, in perfect rhythm, dainty beyond words after her plump elder sister. She knew she looked wonderful in that grey lace dress, the full skirt twisting, twirling as she turned, resting lightly against his arm. There was a curious fire in Martin's grey eyes. But hers were cool, fathomless.

The music ceased. They came to a standstill. Everybody clapped and cheered. Then Jack mischievously called out:

'I say, Martin you fool — look where you've stopped.'

Martin looked up, flushed suddenly as he saw they were just under a bunch of mistletoe. A second he hesitated, then caught his beautiful partner back in his arms. But she, quick as lightning, slipped from them and avoided his lips.

'Too late,' she said, and with a cold smile walked away from him.

He stood staring after her, breath coming quickly, lips grimly set. 'The witch — she makes a man's heart feel on fire. And why should she avoid me — refuse to let me kiss her — on Christmas Eve?' he fiercely asked himself.

Then he shrugged his shoulders and walked back to Carol, who had watched the little scene without much pleasure.

'Come on, darling,' he said. 'Dance this with me.'

She broke into a smile and ran into his arms. He saw her raise her pouting mouth expectantly under that fatal bunch of mistletoe, and he kissed her. But it was without passion or warmth.

He mentally shook himself.

'Idiot,' he muttered. 'You are engaged to Carol. What right have you to want to kiss a stranger like Viva Rhodes?'

She had scored again. She shook with grim mirth as she allowed Chris Miller to dance again with her and thought of that moment when Martin's lips had eagerly bent to hers. She had not let him kiss her. Last year, trembling, dazed, hungry for his kisses, she had been kissed by him, then laughed at by her sisters and friends. To-night nobody laughed — except at Martin.

Nobody, least of all Martin, knew what mad, bitter, passionate memories had flooded upon her when he had caught her in his arms. She had loved him crazily once. She might so easily love him again. But that thought she deliberately erased from her mind. It was for revenge, not for love, she had come to The Grange. And back in Paris the Greek, Basil Rhodes, awaited her; she had promised herself to him — next year.

She shivered suddenly and caught her

lower lip between her teeth. The Miller boy, head over ears in love with her now, looked down at her with infatuated blue eyes.

'You are shivering — are you cold, Miss Rhodes?'

'Not a bit,' she said, casting off the memory of Basil. 'And why be so formal? I've asked all Mary's old friends and relations to call me Viva.'

'It's a beautiful name and suits you,' he said. 'I just don't understand how you ever came to be a friend of poor, dull Mary!'

Viva stiffened, but she continued to smile, to turn the boy's head, whilst mentally registering another grudge against him for his contempt of Mary.

'You would never have fallen in love with her, eh, Chris?'

'Heavens, no! But with you — '

He broke off flushing, stammering, fearing to offend her. She gave a low laugh.

'Silly boy,' she murmured.

Her young sister marched up to them

at the end of that dance. Her pert little face in its frame of red curls was furious. She was not a polished woman of the world and she let Chris see how angry, how jealous she was.

'That was our dance,' she snorted.

'Oh, I am so sorry,' said Viva. 'Mr. Miller, how could you have forgotten?'

She moved away with another musical laugh. Judy stared after her, scowling, then turned back to her sweetheart.

'You did forget and it's as good as making a fool of me in front of Miss Rhodes. What's come over you Chris? That woman seems to be bewitching you.'

'Perhaps you're right,' he said recklessly.

Judy grew white then red.

'Oh!' she said. 'Oh . . . so that creature . . .'

'How dare you be so rude to an honoured guest — a friend of Mary's!' said Chris heatedly. 'And as for calling her a 'creature' — a devinely beautiful, clever girl like Miss Rhodes — you make me laugh, Judy!'

The girl stared at him, then swallowed hard in sheer jealous rage. She marched away from him, her eyes blind with tears, ran straight into the 'creature.' Viva had seen all and been highly amused. She put an arm lightly around Judy.

'Don't look so cross, dear,' she said in her most charming voice. 'Do you know, you've got the loveliest red hair I've ever seen?' She retained the girl, talking to her, in a clever, flattering way. Before five minutes had elapsed Judy had ceased to be jealous or to regard her as a 'creature.' She was irresistibly fascinating, and Judy finally hung on her every word. She even went so far as childishly to confide in Viva about her love for Chris and how rude he was being to-night.

'Never mind,' murmured Viva with a glittering smile. 'Look, child — I see somebody sitting all alone for you to go and be nice to. Mr. — er — what is his name?'

Judy followed her gesture of indication. *It was the bald and elderly Mr. Cortright.*

'That old fossil!' said Judy indignantly.

Viva laughed.

'Another point scored,' she thought. 'My goodness, but revenge is sweet!'

By the end of that evening every woman in the room save Viva Rhodes had been kissed under the mistletoe. But Viva had avoided any kisses. She remained the one and only girl whom any of the men had honestly wanted to kiss.

She went to bed, triumphant, radiant, the complete success, a trifle earlier than the rest; first of all because she was tired, secondly because she knew she would be missed and that the party would fall flat in her absence.

She walked through the deserted hall, a host of memories crowding through her brain. Just then she met the two daily maids going home after washing up all the dishes. Her heart gave a queer leap as she recognised the little one, Alice. The old cook had gone. This was a new one . . . but Alice with her sallow face and tired eyes was very familiar. Viva had a soft spot in her heart for the 'daily.' She had done little services for her in the past — had been the only really kindly one; had perhaps been truly fond of Miss Mary who had done so many jobs in the house to help Alice, whilst Miss Carol and Miss Judy only made work.

Alice stared without recognition at the beautiful young lady who seemed to her like a film star.

'Good evening,' said Viva with her charming smile.

Alice came nearer and twisted a corner of her overall, blushing.

'Oh please, Miss, if you don't mind. I've heard in the kitchen of poor Miss Mary's death and I'm so sorry — I liked her — she was that kind and helpful to me. I've missed her, if I may say so Miss, and I feels sorry now that everyone 'put on her' so, just because she weren't as good-looking as the other young ladies.'

Viva did not speak for a moment. But she had an incredible desire to throw her arms around the little servant's neck and weep out: 'Oh, Alice, Alice, I am Miss Mary . . . ' Alice was the only one whose sorrow was sincere, who had appreciated the good points of that poor, plain Mary Everest. Then she swallowed the lump in her throat. She fumbled in her bag and found a five-pound note. She thrust it blindly into the maid's hand.

'Thank you very much, Alice,' she said huskily. 'This is to wish you a merry Christmas for Miss Mary's sake ...' Alice the little maid stared at the note, then with a gasped, 'Oh God bless you Miss ... ' fled in tears.

Viva Rhodes passed on to her own bedroom, brooding.

'The only one ... the only faithful one — poor Alice! I shall remember that ... she shall have her reward ... and the others ... dear life! How they shall pay!'

Viva stayed at Dene Park a week then took a furnished flat in a big block in Park Lane. It was all part of her scheme that she should dazzle and bewilder her enemies.

The limitless wealth of the Greek who had launched her was at her command, and she spared no money to cause a sensation. The flat she rented was the property of an Indian Rajah now in his native land and was let to Miss Rhodes for a fabulous sum. It was a huge place, furnished in exotic Eastern style and full of gorgeous things which the Rajah had brought from his palace in Delhi.

In this luxurious nest Viva was waited on hand and foot by the finest of servants; a French maid, Jacqueline, and two real Indian servants in turbans who had been left to take care of the flat by their royal master and whom Viva found invaluable.

She had wired, as commanded by Dr. Rhodes before she left, the address of this flat as her headquarters, although he demanded no letters and no account of her doings in London. But within twenty-four hours, a new servant arrived at Viva's flat — from Paris. He was a young handsome Arab boy of great intelligence, and with a gift of music. He could speak English but conversed in French. He threw himself at Viva's feet and laid before her his flute.

'I am to be my lady's personal attendant,' he said humbly, 'to sleep in her shadow, to guard her, to serve her ... '

'Who sent you?' asked Viva, astonished.

'I am a gift from my lord at Amiens.' said the boy, looking at her with great liquid, expressive eyes, 'And my name is Masri.' Viva grew suddenly cold. So the handsome Arab boy was a gift — from Basil. Perhaps not so much a gift as a spy. That thought disturbed and annoyed her. But she dared not send him back. It would insult Basil. All the same she felt that she was not so free as she had imagined. Behind the beauty and music and vows of undying loyalty of Masri she suspected treachery.

From that hour onward he was always with her, at her feet, or outside her door if she dismissed him.

Her next move, after settling in her gorgeous flat, was to issue invitations to the Everests, to Martin Hayle, Chris, the Sharrons, the Page-Ropers and others who had known Mary Everest, for a party to be held at her temporary home which none of them had yet visited.

The invitations were hand-painted, depicting an Eastern scene which aroused the curiosity of the recipients. They accepted with a thrill, and none looked forward to the party, yet dreaded it, more than Martin. For a week he had not seen Viva, he had tried his hardest to be the warm-hearted lover to Carol. And he was finding it difficult, yet he wanted desperately to see Viva Rhodes again.

On the evening before the party, Chris Miller, in the last stages of mad infatuation for Viva — half-crazed because he had telephoned and called and been refused admission — turned up at the Park Lane flat in a dinner-jacket, with a feeble bunch of carnations in his hand. And at last Viva let him come in.

The boy was dazed and overwhelmed by the room into which he was ushered by Masri, the Arab boy. He had seen rooms like this on the films — but never entered such a one. The jewelled lights cast only a dim glow. The room was warm, even hot after the cold January night outside. Through the rich gloom Chris's blue eyes eagerly sought and found Viva. He gasped as he saw her.

She was reclining lazily on one of the divans, her head against a huge peacock-blue cushion. Beside her, on a small lacquer table stood a tray with Turkish coffee and several liqueurs. She was smoking a cigarette in the long holder she generally used, and wore a wonderful dress of white velvet edged with sable and embroidered with silver. It had wide sleeves reaching to the hem of her gown. She wore one priceless sapphire ring and two diamond and sapphire bracelets.

The infatuated boy stumbled forward, careless that Masri was in the room making the coffee. He fell on his knees by the couch, caught up the hand with the ring and covered it with feverish kisses.

'Viva,' he said wildly. 'You've driven me crazy. Oh, my dear, I love you so . . . you wonderful, marvellous creature . . . be kind to me!'

Her dark eyes rested on his bowed

head with a half-contemptuous pity. Then she laughed.

'Don't laugh!' he exclaimed passionately. 'I do love you — I worship you — I want you to marry me.'

'My dear boy!' she drawled. 'Control yourself. You are shocking my Arab boy. Besides, what are you thinking of? You are more or less engaged to Judy Everest.'

Chris moved his head impatiently. 'Judy!' he said.

Inwardly Viva shook with mirth. It was like honey to hear her young sister's name spoken in that tone of indifference, of contempt. Once not so long ago she had heard her name 'Mary' breathed in similar terms. It is delightful to be 'top-dog' when one has been the under-dog for so many bitter years.

'Yes — Judy,' she said gently. 'Such a nice little girl, my dear Chris, and practically engaged to you, surely?'

'Once there was some talk of it,' he admitted. Then he added hoarsely: 'But I couldn't marry her now. She bores me — she's a nice girl — but compared with you — oh, God!'

'Hush, hush,' she said in her sweet, mocking voice, although she did not draw away the slim hand he was so feverishly holding. 'You mustn't be so dramatic, *mon ami*. You are a well-brought-up young man with nice, honourable feelings. You can't throw over your little sweetheart for me, a comparative stranger.'

The boy tried to put an arm around her.

'Viva, Viva, don't tease me, don't madden me with all this nonsense about Judy. I am willing to be friends with her — but I can't marry her now.'

She had eluded his grasp. She lay back on her gorgeous embroidered cushion and looked at him from beneath dark, curling lashes. She picked up a silk fan which lay beside her and began to fan herself lazily. 'My dear Chris, calm down,' she drawled. 'You don't for one moment imagine that you are going to marry me, even if you break with Judy, do you?'

'Yes I do,' he said, with the impudence

and arrogance of extreme youth. 'I adore you. Oh, I know you're rich — that you're a sort of a princess in Greece and all that — but I'm getting on well in the City and I'll work myself to death for love of you, Viva.'

She shrugged her shoulders. Every word he said pleased and satisfied her, eased a fraction of her insatiable and bitter ache for revenge. This was a poor, conceited fool; but once he had grimaced when he had been asked to dance with poor plain Mary Everest. The memory of her humiliation hurt even now, filled her with the hot desire to humiliate him in his turn. Let him babble of his passion and desire for her. She would listen — thirstily drink in every word of flattery, every plea for the mercy she would refuse. She knew her mocking advice to him to go back to Judy and 'be good' would only infuriate him and add to the fuel of his infatuation.

'How old are you, Chris?' she murmured.'

'Twenty-four,' he said. He laid hot lips

against the cool pink palm of her hand. 'But what does that matter, dearest, my most beautiful one?'

'Twenty-four!' she mocked. 'A mere babe. I am a Thousand — from All Time — and the man who loves and wins me shall also be from All Time and a god Immortal.'

It was all said for effect. Chris failed to understand the words and was too desperately in love to analyse or trouble about them.

Once more he pleaded for her love.

He fell on his knees before her and clung to her velvet gown, kissed the fur on it, babbled of his passion. She looked down at him with a sneer on her perfect mouth. He was cringing, feeling himself very small and humble. That pleased her. She could afford to be cruel, to be rude. He would come back . . . she knew it . . . had not the great Basil Rhodes once said to her, in Paris: 'Any man who falls in love with you will be for ever your slave, enthralled, in eternal bondage and the lure of that mouth which I fashioned after the mouth of Psyche, will call your lovers back, back, and back again . . . '

She listened to the distracted boy for a moment, then gave him a languid hand.

'Please go now, Chris — you tire me,' she said.

He rose obediently, tears in his eyes. He looked with passionate longing at the beautiful, unmoved face before him.

'May I come again? May I see you again?'

'Who knows?' she said. 'But you must remember — Judy!'

'I shall tell Judy this evening that I don't intend to marry her, that I don't consider myself bound to her any longer,' he said recklessly.

Viva's heart gave a throb of triumph. Her work was done. She had come between one pair of lovers; she, who had known the bitterness of being alone and unwanted, would make Judy Everest suffer likewise . . . and this poor, conceited, foolish boy learn to yearn for a woman in vain.

'You can do what you choose,' she said

coldly. 'It is nothing to me. Good-night.'

'You will see me again?' he pleaded.

'At my party,' she said indifferently.

'I shall never cease to adore you — to try and make you a little kinder,' he said.

Then, intoxicated by his own burning passion, crazy with thwarted hopes, yet not entirely hopeless, Chris Miller stumbled out of the room.

3

On the night of Viva Rhodes' party to the Everests and their friends, the hostess had planned to surprise and overawe her guests. She succeeded.

A brilliant banquet took place in the dining-room. A long table was spread with gold dishes and sparkling cut-glass goblets. Six women — experienced, attractive girls, dressed as slaves — served the food which was of the most rare and delicate kind.

Masri played to the guests through most of the meal, and when he grew tired there was music from a hired orchestra. No expense had been spared. The whole scene was beautiful, glittering, and it dazzled the Dene Park crowd as they were meant to be dazzled, left them gasping, marvelling, thrilled and almost scared.

All the women had come in their best, latest frocks . . . Carol in pink tulle; Judy in powder-blue; Mrs. Tom Sharron in white lace; Mrs. Roper in brocade. Yet one and all they felt shabby and out of place. But at the head of the table the triumphant Viva sat in state, presiding over that banquet like a princess and looking one — the most brilliant, beautiful woman in that room. She wore a gown which had been specially designed for her in Paris. It was made completely of the iridescent wings of some tropic beetle sewn onto thin guaze, and clung to her slim lovely figure closely, showing every adorable curve.

Whenever she moved the wings flashed and sparkled. The effect was electric. About the slender milky throat was a close-fitting collar of exquisite emeralds, and she wore emeralds in her ears and one great flawless stone on the first finger of her right hand.

She had received her guests in the drawing-room, rich lights throwing a sombre, mysterious radiance upon everything, and she, like a glittering, sinuous figure rising out of the scented dusk to welcome every person who arrived.

It was, they felt, like a film set and they were actors and actresses taking part in the play. She had begun by making an effect, by startling, winning admiration and envy from the women — and more from the men.

When Martin Hayle had first seen her, bent over her hand, looked at her, perfect and exquisite in her own fascinating environment, he had felt a thrill that was fiercely passionate, a fear and dread that he could neither understand nor define. He only knew that she was the most marvellous woman he had ever seen and that once he had entered the portals of her home, Carol became a nonentity, ceased to exist. He hung on her words, could not tear his gaze from her, was conscious at odd moments of vague shame, of the remembrance that he was engaged to be married to Carol.

Now, at the banquet he sat beside her, on her left, whilst Mr. Everest occupied the chair of honour on her right, never dreaming that this mysterious and peerless creature was his own flesh and blood. He was not a conversationalist at the best of times, but fortunately for him Viva did not demand his attention. She spoke nearly all the time to the man on her left.

She had swung from one extreme to the other. Last time she had seen Martin Hayle she had ignored him. To-night she paid him marked attention. The wretched Chris Miller was put at the other end of the long glittering table next to the equally wretched Judy, who believed Viva had arranged this out of kindness but was piteously aware that Chris did not want to be next to her, but stared eagerly up the table at his hostess during the entire meal.

Viva was exerting all her charm, all her influence on Martin now. She knew quite well how he struggled with himself, how he fought to remain faithful to Carol. But she gave him little chance to think or fight, bewildered him by her smiles, her soft, seductive voice, her magnificence. He scarcely ate any of the dishes set before him. Deadly pale, grey eyes smouldering, he sat back in his high carved chair, watching Viva, listening to her, feeling himself irresistibly drawn to her. So must have felt the mythological sailors, lured to the rocks by the voices of the sirens.

Carol, at the beginning, enjoyed her evening, was interested and excited by all the theatrical beauty and novelty of the banquet and the display of wealth. But gradually she was forced to the horrid realisation that for Martin she did not exist. To begin with she was not near him. She had been put at the other end between Tom Sharron and another Dene Park man whom Viva had known in the past. But Martin only looked down at her once ... then in a troubled distracted way, and after that she saw his gaze riveted upon Viva.

She grew sulky and annoyed. She was not going to have Viva Rhodes stealing her Martin. When Carol was annoyed she became 'catty.' During dessert she whispered to Tom:

'All a bit too much like a stage show,

isn't it? And Viva looks as though she ought to have a leopard at her feet.'

She got no satisfaction from Tom who, forgetting that he was Sheila's bridegroom, fatuously answered that Miss Rhodes was the most marvellous creature he had ever seen and that the dinner was beyond compare . . .

The man on the other side of Carol was equally fatuous. Sullen, uneasy for her happiness, Carol stared up at Viva's end of the table.

'She's bewitching everybody,' she muttered.

And was just in time to see Martin hand Viva a nectarine which he had just peeled for her with a look on his pale handsome face that Carol had never seen there. And she grew more than ever afraid for herself.

'Are you enjoying it, Martin?' Viva was murmuring, leaning her elbow on the table and cupping her chin on one palm of her slender hand. 'Or do you feel as I do, that it would be better to be in a garden under the stars . . . alone? . . . '

Her voice sank to a whisper. Martin stared into her great dark eyes and was lost in their witchery.

'Alone — with you — yes — I would like that,' he muttered, and drank a great deal of ice-cold champagne which one of the slave-girls poured into his goblet.

She smiled strangely.

'Sometimes our wishes are granted Martin,' she said in her low mysterious voice.

'What do you mean?' he said almost roughly.

'Listen,' she whispered.

Masri was singing to the accompaniment of his flute. A passionate French song, only half-understood by most of that semi-educated audience, but which Viva knew Martin the Oxonian could translate.

'For like pale wine that flames in a
    lucent cup,
Thy beauty maketh mad my heart and I
Could kiss thy life away, thou Very
    Dear

*Who to my mouth thy mouth doth
 render up!'*

Viva's eyes met and held the questioning grey ones of the man whom she
was slowly driving to madness, who was
every second awakening more poign-
antly to the realisation of a deathless,
devastating passion for her. He tried to
drag his gaze from her, to look at Carol,
but could not.

Viva lifted her goblet to her lips.

'Is the room too hot for you — you are
so pale,' she said with a tinkling laugh.

'You are a witch — a sorceress,' he
whispered hoarsely.

'Foolish Martin,' she whispered back,
with a smile that made his heart shake
with its terrific beating.

When the long dinner came to an end,
Viva led her guests back to the drawing-room and seated them all on divans
in a circle. She had prepared a princely
entertainment for them. As she passed
into the room on Martin's arm, she
brushed against Chris, who had waited

for her.

'Viva,' he said pulling her hand. 'Viva — grant me one moment alone please.'

'I'm busy, Chris,' she broke in, her lips hardening. 'Go back to Judy.'

'You're a beautiful fiend,' he choked. 'I — I — '

But she brushed past him, and sank onto her own divan, bidding Martin sit beside her. Bitterly Chris stared at them, primitive passionate jealousy raging within him. But he was forced to do as she said, to return to the side of the girl who no longer held a fraction of his interest.

Carol, sulky and with untidy golden hair, marched up to her fiancé.

'Come and sit by me, Martin,' she commanded.

'I'm afraid you must be separated from your — er, Martin — just for this evening, Carol,' said Viva very sweetly. 'I can't allow engaged or married couples to sit together. I have arranged all the places for a special reason. You are over there by Jack Spencer, my dear.'

Carol literally ground her teeth. Viva, with an amused look at her turned to Martin, who was flushed and ill-at-ease, smoking the cigar Masri had just given him.

'Would you rather go and sit with Carol?' she asked.

He looked up swiftly, then down again.

'I'm quite happy here,' he muttered.

Carol marched away, with black hatred of Viva in her heart. And Viva sank back on a huge orange cushion, her marvellous iridescent frock glittering in the dim light of the sombre room. She laughed softly.

'So you — like being with me, eh, Martin?'

'You know I do,' he said breathing fast. 'But I don't want to . . . don't you realise what you are doing?'

'What?' she asked, mockingly.

'Making me forget my promise to Carol — driving everything from my brain but you — you — you!'

Triumph gleamed in her eyes. So

she was winning hands down . . . Martin Hayle was falling, falling . . . could not hold out much longer against her potent attack on the strongholds of his heart. Whatever he had been in the past, to-night he was crazily, utterly her own. She could laugh aloud for sheer delight. But instead she went on mocking, luring, inviting him with dark eyes and sweet red lips.

Suddenly all the lights in the room went out. An arc-lamp flashed a circle of lights in the centre of the guests and a young ballet dancer, with a chaplet of roses about her head, sprang into the light and began to dance.

Everybody ceased talking and breathless attention was given to the dance. In the darkness Martin's hand felt for Viva's, found it and pressed it convulsively. She felt a queer electric thrill at the hard pressure of those fingers, but although her slender fingers clung about his, she derided the dangerous emotion that the contact inspired in her. She did not love this man, she did want his love.

She was leading him on only to laugh at him and destroy him.

This was revenge . . . revenge . . .

The dancer vanished, blowing kisses to the delighted audience. Then one of Viva's Indian servants — a juggler and acrobat — leaped into the limelight and began to twist his sinuous brown body into incredible shapes, amidst a burst of applause. Viva was providing a first-class entertainment such as the Dene Park crowd expected to see only in a West End theatre.

But Martin was blind, deaf and dumb to the show. In the shadows he sat on the divan close to Viva, his lips perilously close to the fragrance of her hair, his hand holding hers in throbbing silence. And he knew beyond doubt that there was no other woman in the world for him — but this woman.

Suddenly, with a little stifled laugh, the beautiful fiend leaned closer to him.

'Martin,' she whispered, 'if this foolish juggler bores you, let us slip away. Nobody will see us or miss us in the darkness.'

His heart leaped.

'May we? Oh Viva — ' he whispered passionately.

She rose from the divan, pulling at his hand and led him through the rich gloom of the darkened room to the flower-scented dining room, which was now absolutely deserted. And nobody saw them go — except Masri who was the ever watchful.

For a moment Martin stood hesitant in that bright room, his eyes dazed after the darkness. Then he looked down at Viva. She stirred towards him, her winged frock flashing. Her face was alluring, her dark eyes soft, inviting, her lips a terrible temptation to the man on whom she had exerted her charm the whole of the evening.

'Well,' she murmured.

He doubled his hands, even now striving to fight against her. 'Witch!' he said hoarsely. 'Are you human or an enchanted princess out of a fairy tale?'

She laughed.

'You like me, Martin?'

'Like you? I love you — adore you,' the hot words broke out uncontrollably. 'I know what it means to love and to want — '

'But Carol?' she mocked.

He drew a hand across his eyes.

'You make me forget Carol — everything.'

'Does it matter?' she said, triumph gleaming in her beautiful eyes. 'Don't you want to love me, Martin?'

'If you will love me, Viva, I shall be more deliriously happy than any man in the world.'

'Supposing I tell you that I — don't!'

'I shan't believe you,' he cried. 'You do care — I've seen it in your eyes, on your lips these last few hours. You do love me and I love you. Tell me so — tell me, in my arms.'

He was swept away on the wings of passion now. He caught her blindly in his arms, crushing the delicate opalescent gown, holding her in a throbbing embrace that robbed her of breath. She hung in his arms, motionless, staring up at him a moment. And now she was deathly white and fear rather than triumph gleamed in her eyes.

'Don't kiss me,' she said.

But he did not hear her. He had bent his handsome head and covered her lips with his mouth. During that long kiss she felt her senses slipping from her, her hard, ice-cold desire for revenge thawing into a warmer desire — for him — the old, passionate love reawakening under the passion of his kiss. She tried desperately to recover her equilibrium, to remember why she had tempted this man; what she had meant to do. But she felt momentarily impotent — conscious only of the thrilling rapture of his embrace.

But sinister shadows were gathering round them . . . Masri the Arab, cunning, vigilant on behalf of his master, the Greek, had watched the growing passion between them. Noiseless as a cat he crept up to the divan where Chris Miller sat in sullen silence, and put a hand on his shoulder.

'Come with me,' he whispered. 'S'sh . . . Not a sound . . . but would you see my lady?'

Chris drew a sharp breath and gained his feet. He thought the Arab had come from Viva to lead him to her, that she was going to be kind. All the evening he had sat sullen, jealous, furiously watching her weave her spell over Martin Hayle. For Martin he felt insensate hatred, yet once they had been at school together . . . good friends . . .

He followed Masri through the shadows. The rest of the guests were still engrossed in the entertainment . . . a trio of ballet dancers were now in the limelight.

Masri led Chris out of the room to the doorway of the dining-room.

'Look,' he said, a malicious smile on his evil face. Chris stared through the half-open doorway. He went red then dead white as he saw Viva locked in Martin's arms. They did not see him — Martin's back was turned to Chris — his head bent to that of the girl, her white arms locked about his throat. Masri slid something cold and bright into Chris's hand. The boy, shaking with passionate jealousy and disappointment, stared down at the object . . . saw that it was a toy gun. Then he looked at Martin and Viva again and lost control. The sight of the woman who had driven him half-mad, in the arms of another man, sent him temporarily insane.

He raised the little revolver and fired blindly . . .

In the other room the sharp reports were heard above the sound of the music. The dancers stood still, abruptly. Tom Sharron, who knew a revolver shot when he heard one, leaped to his feet.

'Good God! What's that?' he exclaimed.

Somebody switched on all the lights . . . and three of the company were missing . . . Viva Rhodes, Chris Miller, and Martin Hayle.

Then Carol gave an hysterical scream.

'What's happened? Somebody's been shot . . . Oh, what's happened?'

Judy said hoarsely:

'Where's Chris?'

'And Martin?' added Carol, clinging to Tom Sharron. Judy rushed toward the door and everybody followed her. The dancers were ignored, the orchestra was too scared to go on playing. But before Judy could open the door Masri appeared. He had done his treacherous work on behalf of his absent master. Now he hastened to do the bidding of his mistress. He bowed to the frightened guests and said, 'My lady wishes you to go on with the party. There is no cause for anxiety. There has just been a little accident.'

'To whom? What?' demanded Carol.

'Mr Hayle,' said Masri in his silky voice. 'He and my lady and Mr. Miller were examining a little silver revolver and none knew that it was loaded. Mr. Hayle has a slight wound in his left arm, but is quite all right.'

'Quite all right indeed!' said Carol, now completely hysterical. 'And Martin's been shot. I'm going to him . . . Let me pass, at once . . .'

Masri shrugged his shoulders and stood aside. Carol, followed by her younger sister, rushed into the next room. The rest of the guests stood hesitant — then the lights went out, the music commenced again and the dancers sprang gracefully into the circle of light. Whatever the feelings of the Dene Park crowd, they found themselves baffled and more or less forced to sit down again and continue with the entertainment. But there was an undercurrent of curiosity concerning Martin's accident, and dissatisfaction.

'Extraordinary thing,' muttered Tom Sharron. 'Why weren't those three here, watching the show?'

'Like to know what Hayle's people'll say,' whispered Jack Everest.

'It's awful — I feel all creepy — I'm sure that Greek woman is dangerous,' said Sheila Sharron with a little shiver.

In the dining-room Carol and Judy were met by the extraordinary sight of Martin lying on a pile of cushions, deadly pale, eyes closed, coat off and shirt-sleeve rolled up. His left arm was streaming with blood. Viva Rhodes in her beautiful, shimmering gown was on her knees beside him, with a basin of water and a sponge, attempting to staunch the flow. She was as pale as he, but absolutely composed. The flustered, shattered person in that assembly was Chris Miller — Chris who had brought about the little tragedy. He stood on the other side of the friend he had shot, staring down at him with blue eyes full of horror and a sensation of nausea.

The Everest girls cried out together.

'Oh, Martin . . .'

Instantly Viva was on her feet, facing them, her lovely head thrown back.

'Please don't make a fuss and cause any further disturbance,' she said in a cold, calm voice. 'It was a most unfortunate accident. We three were tired of the dancers and I brought Mr. Hayle and Mr. Miller in here to show them some old firearms. Amongst them happened to be a little jewelled automatic and nobody knew that it was loaded. Mr. Miller was laughing and handling it and it went off — unfortunately caught Mr. Hayle in the arm.'

Carol rushed to Martin's side, flopped on her knees by him. Almost immediately the pink tulle of her frock became dyed a deeper, more sinister red. Judy shuddered and walked up to Chris — caught his arm.

'Chris,' she said, her voice quivering, 'Chris, how awful!' He took not the slightest notice of her, but went on staring at Martin, whose eyes remained closed. He had come to his senses. The moment of madness when his fingers had closed over the revolver which Masri had handed him had passed. He was no longer burning with crazy jealousy. He was appalled at what he had done. He had shot Martin . . . Martin his school friend . . . it was a terrible thing. Curiously enough he bore Viva no malice. She was still the goddess, the woman of his desire. And she had been wonderful. When Martin had been shot, sagged, with her arms around him, she had acted speedily. She had shown no hysteria, never uttered a cry. Swiftly she had placed cushions under the wounded man and set to work to stem the flow of blood from his arm. And while she worked she had said: 'I realise what has happened. But hold your tongue, you foolish boy, and leave things to me . . . pretend it was an accident . . . I'll bear you out.'

'Of course it was an accident,' had been Martin's only words just before he had collapsed.

And that was sporting — decent of him, the wretched Chris reflected. He knew that Martin knew that it was no accident . . . but of course they all wanted to save scandal . . . for Viva's sake.

Carol from her crouching position looked up at Viva. 'Look how he's bleeding! Somebody ought to fetch a doctor.'

'One of my Indians went for a doctor five minutes ago,' said Viva.

Then the doctor arrived.

Martin opened his eyes while the surgeon was examining his arm, groaned a little, then looked round him with dazed eyes. He saw Viva first — a lovely, motionless figure, her dark eyes; fixed on him; then Carol tearful, dishevelled at his side, and Judy at a distance. Then he remembered what had happened. Chris had shot him, put an end to that wonderful thrilling moment when he had held Viva in his arms and felt her lips warm and yielding under his kisses. Accident, or no accident, Martin knew what was expected of him and rose manfully to the occasion.

'Rotten accident . . . just fooling about . . . you understand, doctor?'

The doctor, an elderly man with a large practice in this wealthy neighbourhood, knew when to hold his tongue.

'I quite understand,' he said discreetly. 'There is no serious damage . . . I must just extract the bullet . . . feeling sickish and faint I daresay . . . you've lost a good deal of blood . . . now if we can carry you to a bedroom.'

'Yes my two Indians can take him . . . there is plenty of room . . . he can go to one of the spare rooms,' said Viva.

Later Martin was comfortably installed in a luxurious blue-and-gold bedroom, lying on a soft divan bed, the two servants waiting on him hand and foot. He was feeling better, although still very weak. The doctor had extracted the bullet and bandaged the arm, and advised him to remain where he was for the night. For one moment Viva came in to see him.

He put out a hand and stared at her with a passion of worship in his eyes.

'Viva,' he whispered. 'Viva — my darling — '

'Hush,' she broke in, controlling the desire to fling herself at the side of the bed and bury her head on his arm. 'You must not excite yourself. Besides, you must remember — Carol.'

'After that fatal kiss?' He gave a short laugh. 'No — I don't belong to Carol any more. I belong to you and you to me.'

'You mustn't be so mad,' said Viva biting her lip. 'For heaven's sake, think what your relations, your friends downstairs will have to say about this . . .'

116

'I understand, my dearest, and you shall not suffer through scandal,' he said tenderly. 'But once I am out of here I shall break my engagement with Carol.'

She could not trust herself either to encourage him or argue the point. She said: 'Lie still and remember that you are very weak. Do you wish to see Carol?'

He pulled her hand to his lips. She felt them hot and feverish on her cold palm. A wave of scarlet dyed her beautiful face and throat. She pulled her fingers away almost roughly. 'Martin, you must be sensible. What am I to do? Your people must be informed. Your father; Aunt Ida —'

She broke off, her eyes dilating. In her nervy state she was off her guard. She had forgotten that as Viva Rhodes she was not supposed to know that Mrs. Hayle was dead and that Miss Ida Hayle, a maiden-aunt, lived with Martin and his father. To her relief, however, Martin did not notice the slip.

'Ring them up,' he said. 'Just explain about the accident and say I'll be home in the morning.'

'They may dash round here.'

'No — Aunt Ida is laid up with a chill and Father won't turn out so late. You can explain — say it was an accident. Viva' — he caught her hand again — 'Viva, it was an accident, wasn't it?'

She gave him a long queer look.   .

'Yes,' she lied. 'Chris had no idea the thing was loaded.'

Martin reflected a moment. Then he said:

'But why did he leave the show ... what made him come in to us ... why did he fire at me?'

'Take my advice and ask no questions.'

He looked up at the perfect, inscrutable face. He did not understand her, he only knew that he adored her.

'I don't care about anything so long as I am with you,' he said with a long sigh. 'And for God's sake don't let Carol come up and mouth over me or it'll send me crazy ... Viva, Viva, don't go without kissing me ...'

But she had gone. The shimmering,

exquisite figure had vanished and he was alone in the warm bedroom. He became conscious of the pain in his arm and of the desire to sleep. He shut his heavy eyes and drifted into semi-consciousness, his brain confused, every thought save that of Viva shut out.

Downstairs Viva had a quick, definite interview with Carol. 'Martin is sleeping,' she said. 'And Dr. Massingham advises that he be left absolutely quiet to-night. I am just going to telephone his father.'

Carol was feeling far from pleased with Viva Rhodes. She felt suspicious — of what she knew not — but she gave her a sullen, jealous look.

'Yes, you had better. Thank goodness the accident was no worse. Shall I tell you the Hayles' number?'

'I know it,' said Viva. Then pulled herself up, frowning. It was the second slip she had made to-night. And this one did not pass unnoticed.

'How do you know it so well?' demanded Carol.

Viva's lips curled into a bitter smile. She could scarcely explain that as Mary Everest she had telephoned to the Hayles' house often . . . but with quick cunning she said, 'Martin gave it to me just now.'

The call was put through. Old Mr. Hayle answered Viva. The news of the accident at Miss Rhodes' party naturally disturbed and worried him. He wanted to come round at once. But Viva assured him that Martin was perfectly all right and asleep and that the doctor had said that he would be well enough to be driven home to-morrow, so Mr. Hayle accepted that. Martin had told him that Miss Rhodes was a charming woman and a great friend of 'poor Mary's.' That seemed sufficient. He thanked her for taking care of his boy. He would be round in the morning to see him directly after breakfast . . . most unfortunate . . . but of course it could not be helped . . . etc., etc.

Viva returned to Carol much relieved. She saw the necessity now of appearing nonchalant.

'Come along to my room and change

your frock, Carol,' she said coolly. 'You can't appear in that.'

Carol stared down at the pink tulle, which was stained with Martin's blood.

'Oh — it's horrible,' she muttered. 'I'm going home. I don't want to stay.'

'Pull yourself together, Carol,' said Viva in a firm voice. 'You will cause far more disturbance by making a mountain of it. I have a pink frock upstairs. Jacqueline will put you into it . . . Nobody will notice . . .'

Carol wilted and wavered under the stronger personality. And finally allowed Jacqueline to take off the ruined tulle dress and put her into one of Viva's beautiful frocks. Even after what happened Carol was still feminine and vain enough to be thrilled by the new gown which was ten times more chic and expensive than her own, and Viva had coolly taken the stained tulle and placed it on the fire — given Carol the other in exchange. Carol liked a 'good bargain.'

'Thanks very much,' she said in a mollified tone.

She was almost friends with Viva again when finally they joined the party in the drawing-room, where there was a considerable amount of unrest and discussion. The moment Viva appeared, the guests crowded round, questioned her. The entertainment had ended; the room had been cleared for everybody to dance in and the lights were full on. Viva assumed an air of careless gaiety.

'Such bad luck, the stupid accident,' she murmured. 'But there's nothing to worry about — Mr. Hayle is resting — and he begs us to go on with the dance.'

She suceeded in setting everybody at ease. The shooting incident was half-forgotten and couples began to dance. But Chris Miller had disappeared and did not return that night, and Judy sat sulking in a corner and refused to dance. The rest of the entertainment provided by Miss Rhodes fell rather flat and ended earlier than anticipated. The Everests and their friends retired to their various homes somewhat bewildered.

Later that night Viva stole to Martin's bedroom and stood looking down at the man whose downfall she meant to accomplish. Deliberately she steeled herself against him. How young, how boyish his pale face looked in the dawnlight which was filling the bedroom and dimming the glow of the electric lamp. His dark hair was ruffled, was black against the white of the pillow. And suddenly, as though becoming conscious of the fragrant presence beside him, he opened his eyes. He saw the slender figure in the white velvet dressing-gown; his eyes grew warm and glad.

'Viva — ' he murmured, holding out his right hand.

She did not take it, but smiled down at him.

'You are better? You have slept?'

'Yes, quite all right — but don't be so stiff with me, darling,' he said with a boyish appealing smile that very nearly broke through her reserve. 'Viva, what's the matter? Before that rotten accident you were so different — '

'Hush,' she broke in. 'It is half-past

four in the morning and not the time to discuss things. I am going back to my room. I only came to see how you were.'

Martin stared round him, saw the grey light of morning filling the room with ghostly shadows. Then he put a hand to his head.

'Lord how weak I feel,' he muttered.

'Yes, you must keep quiet and not worry about anything. After your breakfast your father is coming to take you home in your car.'

'I shall tell him that I love you; that I mean to marry you — not Carol Everest,' said Martin recklessly.

'I forbid you to do anything of the kind,' she said in a rapid tone, her cheeks growing hot. 'I have not said I would marry you.'

He stared up at her.

'But — you will,' he said slowly. 'You care for me, Viva. Oh, you couldn't have kissed me like that if you hadn't cared — '

She hesitated an instant, then went on stubbornly with the game she had set herself to play.

'It will be very foolish of you to take seriously what was done in a moment of madness — excitement,' she said.

'But you can't mean — '

'I refuse to talk about it. It is neither the time nor the place,' she said. 'Try and sleep now until you are wakened.'

Martin looked at the beautiful face which was so hard, so implacable this morning, and refused to believe that she meant what she said. She was merely trying to do the right thing . . . the honourable thing . . . for Carol's sake, he reflected. But he would soon make her realise that he would never love or marry any other woman on earth but herself. He resorted to a trick.

'My arm throbs like the deuce — most uncomfortable,' he said, not untruthfully.

Whatever her feeling, she could not bear that he should suffer physical pain. (Such is the peculiar inconsistency of woman!) She moved to his side and bent over him, touched the bandages with slim, delicate fingers.

'What can I do?' she began.

'This,' he said, with a low laugh and caught her round the waist with his uninjured arm, dragged her beautiful head down to his, forced her lips upon his mouth.

For an instant she did not resist — she was shaken with the passionate thrill of it — then with a stifled cry she shook herself free of him, turned and walked out of the room without another word, locked herself in her own room and flung herself face downward on the great gold bed. She did not cry. She just lay there, supine, mentally fighting one of the fiercest battles she had yet fought. Love — versus revenge — a bitter fight — and it had only just begun. When she lifted her head her beautiful face was colourless, the lips Martin had kissed were bitten through.

'Fool — weak, senseless fool!' she derided herself. 'This thing has got to go on in the spirit in which it was commenced, otherwise it will be your downfall rather than his!'

For the moment revenge was stronger

than love. She had won the fight before she slept that fateful night. But she did not know that out in the darkness of the corridor, Masri, the Arab, had watched her enter Martin's bedroom and had seen that single kiss; had attached to it the greatest importance.

'My lady loves the Englishman,' Masri reflected. 'And perchance my master in France would like to hear of this — it grows dangerous!'

Later that same morning Martin Hayle was removed from the big flat in Park Lane by his father. He left reluctantly and without being permitted to bid farewell to his beautiful hostess, who even declined to interview Mr. Hayle. Jacqueline informed father and son that 'Madame' was resting after the party and was not to be disturbed, but would send round to Mr. Hayle's house later in the day to inquire after the injured man. A thousand apologies from 'Madame' for the regrettable accident . . . etc . . . etc . . .

Mr. Hayle drove away from the flat

quite satisfied that Miss Rhodes had been kindness itself to his son and that Martin was not seriously ill — merely suffering from shock and haemorrhage. The old stockbroker was also duly impressed by the grandeur of the flat and the magnificent Indians who assisted Martin into his car, and wrapped him carefully in rugs.

'You've made a pretty wealthy friend my boy,' he said. 'Sorry I didn't see the lady. And, what a good thing that shot got you in the arm and not in the head.'

Martin had little to say. Pale and gloomy, he sat back in the car, feeling really ill with worry and depression, because Viva had refused to see him before he left her home. Why was she treating him like this? Why had she become so cold, so inaccessible after her warm surrender to his kisses last night?

He brooded over the whole affair, and the more he thought of her the more determined he became to make her his wife. He found it impossible to believe that she was playing with him. But for the moment perhaps he had better say nothing of his change of affection to his people. Let them go on regarding him as Carol's promised husband. He felt he could not face Carol just now, however. He wrote her a hasty note when he arrived home to say that he was much better but unable to see her or have any visitors until he was stronger.

That would keep her away, he thought grimly . . . then . . . as soon as he was well enough to get out he would go straight to Viva Rhodes and claim her for his own.

But the first person to see Viva after that dramatic night of the party was the unhappy Chris.

He called at the Park Lane flat shortly after Martin had quitted it. Viva received him. She wanted to see him, to put an end to what she called 'hot-headed folly.' If Chris had expected to see a languishing, exotically-dressed siren he was mistaken and astonished. Viva, on this cold, brisk, bright winter's morning, was in tune with the elements.

He was shown into a small ante-room

which he had not seen before; a sunny little room, furnished in exquisite taste with Queen Anne furniture — somewhat more Spartan and English than the huge Oriental drawing-room. Viva stood by the window — quietly, elegantly dressed in a severely-cut dark green suit, with a beautiful sable fur about her throat and a small green hat with coq-feathers sweeping over the brim. She looked pale. Chris advanced towards her, feeling nervous, as he would have felt in the presence of royalty. Viva gave one that sensation this morning.

'Well?' she said, breaking the silence.

'Viva,' he said huskily. 'I . . . my God . . . I've suffered terribly all night. I haven't been to bed.'

She looked at him — recognised the signs of anguished remorse on his haggard young face, of bitter longing in his nice blue eyes. She had meant to be stern and scornful. She relented — found herself speaking to him very gently.

'I am sorry Chris.'

He seized one of her hands, kissed it.

She could feel the kiss burn through one of her delicate suede gloves. She drew the hand away, still very gentle with him.

'No use my dear,' she said. 'You had far better have done with all this sentimental, tragic business.'

'You mean you love Martin Hayle,' he said in a harsh voice.

She was amazed and angry with herself for flushing scarlet from throat to brow.

'Not at all,' she said curtly. 'I love no man. I do not intend to marry any man.'

'But you were in his arms last night — you were kissing him — and you never let me kiss you — ever!'

She looked down at the ground, biting her lip. She hated to be reminded of that passionate embrace — dreaded lest she should break down and tell this foolish boy that he was right — that she did love Martin Hayle — had always loved him — was Mary Everest — the despised, ugly Mary. Instead she said:

'That is not your affair. And I beg you not to make anything concerning me your affair. Last night you did a terrible thing — very nearly brought about your friend's death. He is at home now with no worse than a flesh wound in his arm. But let it be a warning. Go back to Judy, Chris.'

He stumbled to a chair and hid his ravaged face in his hands. 'Good heavens!' he moaned. 'I know I nearly killed him. I must have been crazy. It was seeing you — in his arms.'

'Where did you get that revolver?' she asked in a voice of deadly coldness.

'Masri, the Arab boy gave it to me.'

Viva's beautiful eyes glittered . . . then she nodded. 'Ah!' she said, as though confirming some suspicion she had been fostering.

He looked up at her.

'Viva, Viva, forgive me, be kind to me — I can't bear much more,' he said hoarsely. 'You're driving me mad.'

'You drive yourself mad,' she said. 'You men are such poor, weak fools. You can jeer at an ugly woman — resist her easily enough. But you cannot resist a beautiful or fascinating one. It makes me laugh.'

'You can afford to laugh,' he said brokenly. 'You are the victor. I am the vanquished.'

Once again pity knocked at the heart of the girl who had come to England to take her revenge. She came to the boy and laid a hand on his arm.

'Chris, I don't want your love,' she said. 'I want your friendship if you care to give it to me.'

He snatched at that crumb of comfort like a starving man; caught the hand and held it against his heart.

'Viva, you mean that? Oh, Viva, I'll do anything to please you — if you will just be kind.'

'Very well, we will be friends,' she said, a trifle impatiently. 'And there are two things you must do, to start with. One is to come only when I ask you; the other to be as sensible as you can and not make Judy too unhappy.'

'You're an angel,' he said hysterically. 'Last night you seemed to me a beautiful friend; but this morning you prove your-self an angel.'

Long after he had gone, Viva Rhodes stood like a statue, staring out of the window, thinking things over. An angel! She who had almost broken the boy's heart and brought about a serious trag-edy — the death of Martin — she was deliberately and wickedly revenging her-self on all these stupid people who had once made her so unhappy! *An angel.* That heaped coals of fire on her head.

She sighed bitterly. She was not very happy in her triumph. Yet to-day she had won another victory. She had made Chris her friend — made him promise to be 'kind to Judy.' That would bring Judy to her feet again. She was all-powerful. She could do what she chose with every one of them.

Then she remembered what Chris had told her. Masri had given him that automatic. Her lips grew hard, her slen-der body shook with anger. Yet she dared not send for him and accuse him of it. She knew why he had done it . . . knew that he was secretly watching over her on behalf of his master . . . the one being who was more powerful than herself.

She shuddered and suddenly walked out of the room — out of the flat — into the cold, sunlit street. She wanted to walk, to shop, to get away from her ugly thoughts . . . thoughts which made her afraid of unknown things . . .

For the present, at least, she would leave Chris Miller alone. He had suffered enough. But Martin Hayle . . . ah, what of him? His punishment had only just begun . . . his and Carol's.

Two days later Viva waited for Martin as she had waited for Chris, in the curiously chilling, austere atmosphere of the Queen Anne boudoir. He had telephoned to say that the arm was better and that he was coming to see her.

When he saw her — this afternoon in a severe grey velvet dress with delicate Spanish lace at throat and wrist — he thought how perfect, how adorable she was; more adorable, because so simple, so girlish, than in her bizarre evening gowns. Yet the moment he looked down into her eyes he felt curiously chilled. She was frozen, regal — small, glossy brown head proudly poised on the slim white throat. She motioned him to a chair.

'Sit down, Martin,' she said. 'You don't look very fit yet.'

He stood before her, grey eyes smiling, although his face was drawn, his arm in a black sling.

'I'm all right. Going strong. Doctor's very bucked with the way the wound is healing. I had to see you, Viva.'

Her delicate brows contracted.

'Sit down,' she said again.

'No,' he said. 'I'm not going to obey you. I'm going to risk your wrath by doing — this!'

He caught her round the shoulders with his right arm and drew her against him. She gasped, baffled by the unexpectedness of it. As she felt the hard beating of his heart against her breast, she thrilled and trembled. It was going to be difficult to punish this man whom she loved . . . wanted . . . difficult to resist the boyish, open charm of him. He was not a weakling like Chris . . . he was a strong, sane, clean-minded man in love with her and believing in her.

'Let me go, please, Martin,' she pleaded.

'No,' he said. 'No — I love you — I adore you — I must kiss you. For days and nights I have thought of that kiss. I paid for it, I know . . . but I would pay and pay again. Viva, beloved, kiss me . . . kiss me . . . '

She tried to elude his eager lips.

'No, no, Martin — let me go!'

'Don't turn your beautiful head away, dearest,' he besought her. 'Look at me, listen to me. Ah, darling, why try to fight against our love? It is strong — too strong for you or me to resist.'

She knew that he was right — that he was breaking down her reserve, that she was weakening again. She made one final effort to push him away. Then he gave a cry of pain — she had hurt his injured arm in her confusion.

She heard the little indrawn breath of pain — saw him whiten and he released her. At once her heart over-flooded with remorse, with tenderness. She was no longer the fiend of revenge — she was all woman, honest, tender, adoring. She took him in her arms and drew his handsome head down to hers.

'Martin, Martin, my dearest, I've hurt you!' she muttered. 'And I love you — love you so!'

She was caught to his heart again. Radiantly he smiled down at her flushed beautiful face.

'Then you do, you do love me, beloved . . . '

'Yes,' she said recklessly. 'Yes, I do . . . '

But before his lips touched her mouth, somebody opened the door. She gave a little start and stared over Martin's shoulder. Then her face blanched. Her knees shook beneath her. For framed in the doorway was the great, powerful figure and curly head of the last man on earth she wished to see . . . the man who had given her beauty, riches, power . . . the

man to whom she belonged . . . Basil
Rhodes.

4

With a swift movement Viva disengaged herself from the arms of the man she loved.

'Basil!' she exclaimed.

Martin swung round. For a few seconds there was silence while the two men sized each other up. The Englishman and the younger of the two was flushed, bright-eyed, still thrilling from the kiss of the woman he adored and from the memory of her confession of love for him. The Greek was like a statue, immobile, frozen, eyes as hard and cold as the glaciers of the North. He was the first to speak. He bowed with old-world courtesy.

'Pardon,' he said. 'I fear I am interrupting an — er — charming idyll.'

Martin gave a short, confused laugh, and glanced at Viva. His was the embarrassment of a thoroughly British young man discovered at an awkward moment by a stranger. She, however, was not the blushing or confused girl he might have expected. She was standing with her beautiful, proud head erect, as cold, frozen as the man who had interrupted the 'idyll.' If she was afraid or angered she showed neither sentiment. She answered Rhodes in the same chilling sarcastic voice in which he had spoken.

'Please don't apologise. But I cannot understand why my servants did not announce you.'

The Greek spread out his hands with an apologetic gesture. But there was no apology in those light, penetrating eyes of his. They seemed to read through Viva's very soul. Her fear deepened, but she smiled.

'Allow me to introduce you — Basil, this is my friend, Martin Hayle. Martin — Dr. Rhodes, from France.'

Martin thrust out a hand with his natural good nature and the boyish manner which was his greatest charm.

'How-do-you-do?' he said. 'I'm delighted to meet you, Dr. Rhodes. You must be a relative of Viva's.'

The Greek merely touched that outstretched hand and bowed again. Behind his icy mask of courtesy and composure he was a seething mass of rage and jealousy. He had come upon these two just in time to hear Viva say that she loved this man, Martin Hayle. He would like to have found himself back in the days when men carried their swords at their sides. In this moment he would have ripped out a blade and struck Martin across the mouth that had dared to touch the lips of the woman he, Basil Rhodes, had created and claimed for his own.

Viva caught her breath nervously, small hands clenched at her sides. Martin was unconscious of the animosity of the other man, but she could feel the cold breath of fury under the doctor's veneer of civility, and she shivered. What had she better do? Martin might blunder ahead in his honest, adoring fashion — tell Basil that he meant to marry her . . . something crazy like that . . . and under the circumstances it would be dangerous. Indeed, she was surprised that Basil did not tell him now, with cold irony, that he was no relative . . . that she had merely used his name to suit her ends . . . that she was *his* promised wife.

But the doctor remained silent, neither denying nor admitting any relationship with Viva. It was impossible for her to fathom his thoughts and intentions. But at all costs she wished to divert a scene between the men.

With quick feminine tact she moved forward and laid a slim white hand upon Basil's arm.

'It is indeed an unexpected pleasure to see you,' she murmured. 'Just ring that bell . . . so . . . now my servants will come and take you to a spare room. You will want a wash . . . take off your coat . . . you have probably just crossed over from France . . . ask for a drink, anything you like . . . I will be with you in one moment. I must just see Mr. Hayle out. He was going when you came.'

The Greek smiled, but for the third time bowed low.

'Pray don't let me drive Mr. Hayle out,' he said amiably 'But I would like to wash — and to have a drink. We will meet again in a few minutes. How well you are looking, *ma chère*. Good-bye — er — Mr. Hayle.'

'Oh — good-bye,' stammered Martin.

He walked out of the little Queen Anne room followed by the two Indian servants. As the door closed upon him, Viva breathed a sigh of relief. But when Martin would have caught her in his arms she stepped back a pace.

'No, no, Martin,' she said breathlessly.

'No? But dearest, why?' he began, his brows puckering.

'Not now — please,' she said. 'I can't explain but . . . but Dr. Rhodes' arrival here makes all the difference.'

'To what? Our love? How can it?'

She bit her under-lip nervously and avoided the frank questioning of his handsome eyes.

'Martin, I can't tell you now. But I beg you to go away. I — I'll write — phone you later — I promise.'

He stared at her. He saw that she was pale and agitated. He had never seen her so before — this regal, cool, self-possessed woman. Why did she want him to depart so hurriedly? Was she afraid of this doctor from France? He was a magnificent-looking fellow, with excellent manners, Martin reflected. But why should his coming make all the difference?'

Viva refused to answer his questions.

'I can't tell you anything now,' she said. 'But if you love me, go away, Martin, until I ask you to come back.'

He walked up to her and took her hand, kissed it with lips that burned.

'Viva, I adore you — you know it,' he whispered. 'I want to please you, to do just what you ask. But I can't help being puzzled . . . and oh, my dear, if you didn't ask me to come back, it would drive me crazy. Viva, you have kissed me, told me you care . . . you meant it, didn't you? You weren't playing?'

'No — I wasn't playing,' she said.

'You will send for me soon — explain this mystery?'

'I can't tell you just when,' she said evasively.

'But you do love me?'

She wanted to throw herself into his arms, to cling to him, to beg him to take her away from this sumptuous flat and all that it meant. Yes, she loved him . . . there was nothing, nobody on earth for her now but Martin . . . Martin whom she had worshipped and hungered for when she was Mary Everest . . . whom she loved a hundred times more dearly now that she had tasted the sweetness of his passion and love. But the thought of the man who had just come from Amiens held her dumb.

'Go now — please, my dear,' she pleaded.

'Before I go just tell me this — what relation is Rhodes to you, Viva?'

'I — oh — my brother,' the lie tumbled out. She had to say something. But she hated having to lie to Martin. He seemed satisfied by the answer. He kissed her hand again, looked down at her exquisite face with unutterable tenderness in his eyes.

'I'll do as you ask and quit,' he said boyishly. 'But don't let it be long before you send for me, my beloved. Remember that I adore you — that I intend to break my engagement with Carol this very evening.'

'No — no, don't!' said Viva.

'I must, Viva,' he said. 'I can't possibly go on pretending to care for her.'

'Well, wait . . . wait till I give you leave,' she said, breathing fast.

'But why?'

'Oh, don't ask any more questions, Martin.'

'More mysteries!' he sighed, shaking his head. 'I must say I can't understand why your brother's sudden arrival should alter everything and — '

'Just go away and trust me,' she broke in.

'There is no true love without trust, Viva,' he said. 'And I love you, love you, Heart of my Heart!'

She felt sudden hot tears sting her eyes. But she dared not let him see them.

She turned her head away.

'You're a dear,' she said unsteadily. 'Good-bye for now. We shall meet again soon.'

After he had gone she experienced a sensation of mingled pain and relief. She walked into her drawing-room, which was richly sombre, jewelled lights already burning. Outside the winter dusk was settling over London. Basil Rhodes was sitting on one of the divans, smoking a cigarette in a long ivory holder which was familiar to her. He had washed and removed his overcoat, and was now immaculate. He rose when Viva came into the room and she stared at him a moment, curiously.

She had forgotten how immensely tall and broad-shouldered he was; how handsome in a curiously sinister fashion with his thick reddish curls and carven features and compelling eyes. Yet she instinctively compared him with Martin; slimmer, more boyish, sun-browned . . . whose eyes were a much warmer, more candid grey, whose mouth was so much more gentle in curve. The gratitude which had been almost a passion with Viva, which she had felt for Basil Rhodes in France after he had given her the beauty she had craved, seemed remote now, secondary in comparison with her overwhelming feelings for Martin.

The Greek, on his part, looked at her and felt his heart leap with triumph once again at the sight of this lovely girl whom he had fashioned. He had thought of her, wanted her since the day she had sailed from Boulogne away from him. Now be realised afresh how perfect she was in her beauty and grace combined with the intelligence of the woman of the world for which he was also responsible. He put down his ivory holder and took both her hands.

'After many weeks,' he said, 'we meet again. May I say that you are more lovely than I had imagined?' His flattery did not stir her. She drew her fingers from his, conscious of irritation at the contact. She could not even feel pleased to see him again. Yet why — why should she have changed in a few short weeks? Was it because her desire for revenge and her malicious delight in hurting those who had hurt her had been submerged in the fire of her reawakened love for Martin? She wanted nobody but Martin. She had no place in her life for this man. And she was sworn to him; had vowed to become his wife at the appointed time! Her beautiful eyes dilated at the thought.

Suddenly she broke into impassioned speech.

'How dared you come, Basil? What right had you to come unannounced like that? You have broken our compact. It was agreed that we should separate for a definite period — that I should have absolute freedom without supervision until that period expired.'

His eyes narrowed to slits.

'That is quite true, Viva. And I admit that I have broken my compact. But only because you have broken yours.'

'What do you mean?'

'It is obvious,' he said. 'What I saw when I came into your boudoir a few minutes ago was direct proof that you have broken your word.'

She flushed hotly, but flung back her head.

'And what was my word?'

'You know,' he said. He gripped her delicate wrist with vice-like fingers. 'You belong to me, I made you. You swore to return to me.'

'Who said I would not return?'

'That is a quibble. Do you think *I* wish to marry a woman who has given many kisses and caresses to another man?' he asked darkly.

She felt a sudden fury of resentment — wrenched her wrist from his fingers. The delicate Spanish lace tore in the action but she did not notice it. Her dark eyes blazed up at the doctor.

'You have not played fair!' she panted. 'You have spied on me. How did you know I was giving kisses — or caresses — to any man? Through Masri, that horrible, treacherous little Arab boy!'

Basil folded his arms on his chest. He shrugged his massive shoulders.

'That may be so. Masri is in my employ and was my present to you. Surely you cannot find a child so beautiful — horrible?'

'The beautiful child is a spy!' she said accusingly.

'Had you kept your bargain and played fair with me, my spy would not have troubled you,' he said in a silky voice.

She moved her head impatiently, walked to one of the lacquer tables and took a cigarette from a gold box. Basil at once sprang to her side and lit it for her. She smoked in silence a moment and he watched her pace up and down the softly-lit room. When he next spoke to her his voice was softer, silkier than ever.

'Remember, Viva, that I would not have come to-day had it not been necessary,' he said. 'I gave you a year of freedom. You could have done just what you wanted . . . except the one thing . . . give your love, your lips to any man save myself. You are my promised wife — do you forget that fact?'

She paused before him, her large dark

eyes smouldering. She knew that she *had* forgotten. Her slim body shook silently.

'You must release me from that promise, Basil,' she said.

'And why?' He rapped out the words.

'Because I love Martin Hayle,' she said bravely.

She saw the blood sting his face, recede; a look of cold fury gleamed in his light grey eyes and his hands doubled at his sides. But his lips smiled.

'Indeed? That is interesting, *ma chère*! You — love this Englishman who snubbed you, sneered at you when you were Mary Everest and whom you meant to pay back — to make suffer for what he did to you?'

'Yes,' she said breathlessly. 'I can't punish him. I feel just as I used to feel for him in the old days — only more so. You may think me weak, stupid, whatever you like, but I have tried to be cruel — indeed I have been fiendish to everybody. I have hurt my sisters, my friends; particularly Chris Miller. Did you notice that Martin's arm was in a sling? Chris shot him at my banquet the other night. You see, I have driven them to madness, been the cause of bloodshed . . . oh, I have won my victories . . . got my own back . . . but to Martin I cannot do any harm.'

Basil nodded once or twice.

'So!' he said. 'The beautiful fiend becomes the angel — merciful and forgiving.'

'Don't mock me, Basil,' she said, frowning. 'I have not particularly enjoyed my success . . . I have been through several little hells.'

'For that I am sorry,' he said. 'But I do not intend that you put me through any torment, *ma mie.*'

'You are going to keep me to my promise?' She stared up at him, her heart racing furiously, her cheeks ashen.

'Till death!' he said with sudden passion. 'I gave you your beauty and your power and you shall not go to any man's arms save mine. You belong to me, body and soul, and you know it!'

She shrank back from him. The kindly protector, the generous friend, the healing surgeon, seemed to have vanished. In this man before her she could see only a devil — a cold, pitiless devil. And once a woman got into his clutches there would be no release.

'Why should I belong to you?' she said, with a hand to her pulsing throat. 'What right have you to tyrannise over the whole of my life just because you have given me beauty and money? No, no — I won't belong to you. I'll work — pay back the money you have spent on me, do anything to become independent,' she added in a feverish voice.

Basil Rhodes laughed. It was a sinister sound.

'Little fool!' he said. 'You could not pay back in a lifetime of work the thousands I have spent on you, even if I wanted the money. But the money means nothing. It is you I want. It is you I mean to have.'

Viva twisted her hands together and suddenly sank onto the divan behind her. She was weak, trembling. Yet Basil's eyes were not cruel or hard as he looked down at her beautiful bowed head. They were caressing, almost tender. He loved this girl whom he had made into Psyche, Helen of Troy, Venus — all the lovely women of the ages — more than he had ever loved anybody in his selfish, unscrupulous life before.

'Don't be so upset, Viva,' he said. 'After all, when you left Paris you were willing to return to me at the end of the period. You did not find me so — so unacceptable?'

'No — no — you don't understand,' she muttered. 'I was mad with bitterness, with spite ... but now ... '

'You will feel like that again, *ma mie*,' he said. He sat down beside her, took her hands in his own, held them tightly. 'Listen,' he added in a low, compelling voice. 'Don't let your contrition — your tender feelings for this man, Martin, make a weak fool of you. Remember your past injuries — how you were ignored, sneered at, neglected. Remember how your sisters rode over you, laughed at you, how all these Dene Park friends jeered when the man, Martin, kissed you under the mistletoe ... '

He poured out the words cleverly, cunningly, recalling to her every story she had told him of her unhappy life as Mary Everest. He worked on her feelings, her pride, until he almost succeeded in robbing her of the remorse she had been feeling since she had awakened to her love for Martin. She listened to him, still trembling, hesitating, suffering the old agonies of humiliation and bitterness with every incident recalled.

At last she pushed his hands away from her.

'Stop — please stop!' she said hoarsely.

'Well, my Viva?' he murmured, smiling. 'Do you still feel so penitent for taking your revenge? Are you going to let them all off so lightly — just because of an infatuation for this man, Martin . . . ?'

She was strung up to concert-pitch, scarcely in the mood to choose between right and wrong. She flung back her head, flushed, hot-eyed, quivering.

'You belong to me,' he whispered. 'The little lapse with Martin — poof! — what is it?' He shrugged his shoulders. 'You are mine and you know that.'

She stared ahead of her, dark eyes slumbrous, resentful.

'I do not know that I am,' she said very slowly. 'Meanwhile, my dear *brother*,' she gave a short laugh — 'you must find an hotel. You cannot stay here.'

'You do not trust me, *ma mie*? If these people think I am your brother, surely . . . '

'I would rather you did not stay here,' she broke in.

He smiled

'Your wishes are law, *ma mie*. But Irene joins us to-morrow — then we can both stay here, eh?'

'Irene?' Viva frowned. 'Your sister is coming? But why?'

'She has resigned herself to the fact that you are my promised wife and would like to see her future sister-in-law,' said Basil smoothly. 'It will be a charming situation . . . me and my two sisters . . . *eh bien!*'

Viva did not laugh. She was plunged in gloom. She dared not even think of Martin. She only felt that she was in a dark, sinister pool into which she was being pushed, deeper and deeper, by this man . . . that the light of sweet, clean love, of tender impulses would soon vanish for ever . . . and the dark water close for ever and ever over her head. Vengeance was sin. The wages of sin is death . . .

That night Martin quietly but firmly broke his engagement with Carol Everest. He gave no reason save that he had ceased to care for her and considered it his duty to her and to himself to end things between them.

It was a heavy blow to Carol's pride, and in her shallow way she cared more for the handsome young stockbroker whom she had known so many years than for any other man who had wanted to marry her.

She raged at him and pleaded in turns. It was inevitable that she should finally accuse Viva Rhodes of being the cause of the change in her lover's affections. Martin remained mute on the subject of Viva, neither denying nor admitting anything. In the end Carol was quite sure in her own mind that he loved Viva. She flung his ring back at him, enduring much of the bitterness and humiliation Mary Everest had suffered in the past.

'Go!' she told him hysterically. 'Go to your wonderful Viva. But she'll let you down in the end. Everybody says there's something mysterious about her . . . and I bet you're not the first to make love to her, not the last . . . but you'll come back to me in the end — you'll see.'

Martin did not attempt to argue with her; nor to defend Viva. He had not yet been given the right to do that. But his fine grey eyes flashed a little as Carol hurled insinuations at him. Finally he left her to rage alone.

'I'm sorry, Carol,' he said genuinely. 'I hate breaking my word to you, but as I feel like this, it is much better to do so. If we married there would be no happiness for either of us.

Carol took her troubles to Judy, who joined her in bitter accusations against Viva.

'Of course he's infatuated with that

Greek woman, like Chris,' Judy muttered. 'If I were you, I'd go round and tell her what you think of her.'

'I shall!' said Carol, whose pretty face was convulsed. 'I shall go now. I don't care whether her relations from France are there or not — I shall tell her what I think of her in front of them.'

But she was a little afraid of 'the Greek woman,' as she called 'Mary's friend.' And she did not pluck up courage to go round to Viva's flat for several days after Martin had severed the tie between them.

Viva heard of Martin's broken engagement from him by note.

'*I had to do it — forgive me, Viva,*' he wrote. '*Now I am free and when you want me, send for me. I love you and I believe in your love.*'

She read his passionate little note with a feeling of triumph. Then she went to her bedroom and summoned her maid. 'Bring me a mirror, Jacqueline,' she said.

The maid brought her the tortoiseshell-backed mirror from her dressing-table. She stared feverishly at herself. Yes — she was beautiful, loveliness incarnate, and she wanted to taste all the raptures, all the honeyed sweetness life could offer a beautiful woman ... she would defeat Basil, Carol, everybody ... she would gain her supreme triumph.

And how could that be achieved, save through marriage to Martin? If she could arrange to marry him secretly, it would be a terrific victory over this Greek who thought her so completely in his power. Her pride was roused. Her spirit rebelled against Basil. She would marry Martin; then he would never be able to take her from him ... and Carol would never be able to take him, either. Even if Martin found out that she married him half for love, half for revenge, he would be bound to her for ever. It was breaking her promise to Basil ... but she had a right to break it. He wanted to master her, body and soul. She owed him gratitude and allegiance no longer.

Viva drove from her flat to the nearest public call-office. From there, knowing she was safe from the wretched little Arab spy, she telephoned to Martin Hayle.

He came to the telephone and answered eagerly.

'My dearest! How sweet of you to ring me up. I have just been getting into trouble with my doctor. He says my arm is not too good this morning and has bound me to the sofa for the rest of the day. An infernal nuisance!'

Viva's brain worked rapidly. Martin laid up for the day! That meant she must go to his house. She said:

'If I come to your house, is there any chance of seeing you alone?'

'Yes, every chance, darling. Father has gone to the City and Aunt Ida always goes out shopping at eleven.'

'Then may I come round?'

'*May* you!' he said in a passionate voice that left no doubt that he wanted her. 'But what has happened since we met — nothing serious, I hope?'

'I won't say anything on the phone,' was Viva's reply.

At half-past eleven she was at the

Hayles' place and had been shown into the drawing-room — a comfortable, rather conventional and unattractive room full of the venerable Aunt Ida's antimacassars and plants and valuable, hideous china in glass cabinets.

Viva's pulse gave a queer thrill as she entered and looked about her. It was so familiar. Here, as Mary Everest, she had come once or twice in the past to lunch or tea with Miss Hayle. Nothing had changed here, even the two photographs on the mantlepiece were in their old familiar places; one of the late Mrs. Hayle — so like Martin — a beautiful face with serene eyes and dark smooth hair; the other of Martin himself, in his eighteenth year, whilst at college — extraordinarily good-looking, alert, smiling. And now another queer pain throbbed at Viva's heart as she remembered the snapshot of him (at the same age) which she had torn to pieces on that dark, bitter Christmas morning when she had crossed to France.

Martin little realised the thoughts in

her mind as he watched her advance towards him. He was covered with a plaid rug, at right angles to the cheerful fire. His eyes were warm, welcoming.

'My dearest!' he said, in a hushed voice.

The next moment she found herself on her knees by the couch, her arms enfolding him, his about her, and his handsome head was pillowed against her breast.

'Oh my darling, my Viva!' he murmured passionately.

'Do you love me so much, Martin?'

'Madly, desperately,' he said.

'So much that you would — marry me — at once?'

He lifted his head and stared at her, his boyish face alight, his eyes brilliant.

'Viva, you *mean* that?'

'Yes, I mean it,' she said in a strange, excited voice. 'Do you care so much that you would marry me by special licence at a registry-office — say the day after to-morrow — and ask no questions, no reason . . .'

'But you wouldn't do it!'

'I will, if you consent.'

He gave a low cry and strained her against him. She said, 'Oh my dear, be careful of your arm; remember you are an invalid!' but he only held her closer, laughing the gay, glad laugh of a lover.

'I'd marry you this moment if it were possible' he said boyishly. 'Ask no questions. Only give me the right of a husband to protect you, to love you — it is all I ask.'

Her heart beat fitfully, her pulse raced. As she looked at him, at his transfigured face, she asked herself if she had any mortal right to do this thing for the sake of revenge — even though she loved and wanted him. Yet she really, genuinely loved him, was grateful for his love and adoration of her. In that respect she would give him what he gave . . . never let him down.

She pictured him making this mad, unrestrained love to the Mary Everest of the past, and could have laughed aloud with the thrill, the triumph of it.

Then Martin sobered down a moment — passed from his delirium to practical thought.

'How can I marry you?' he asked gloomily. 'I earn £1,800 a year and get £500 from my father. What is that to a woman so enormously rich as you, Viva? Even when the dear old man dies, I shall only have £3,000 a year for life. That is nothing to you.'

'Don't talk of money,' she said breathlessly. 'I can give that up, but in any case, I want you to make me your wife — I beg you to.'

'You — to beg to me — and that!' he was shocked, horrified. He drew the white suede gloves from her slender hands and kissed them, then kissed her finger tips, each one in turn. 'You are a goddess to me,' he added.

She was silent. Anguish appeared in her dark, beautiful eyes. She was going back, back, to the memory of that conversation she had overheard on Christmas Eve between Carol and this man, when he had said, 'The poor girl looked so forlorn, I felt sorry for her. I assure you I didn't want to kiss her . . . '

And now he wanted to marry her.

Before she had left the Hayles' house, she had gained all that she had wanted; his promise to remain on his couch and rest; to meet her in two days' time at the Marylebone Registry Office and marry her secretly. He was content to do her least bidding, to keep her secret, even to part from her after their marriage and say nothing until she gave him leave. He was utterly in love — utterly her slave.

Yet the look on her face as she drove to Somerset House to apply, on Martin's behalf, for a special licence, was tragic rather than rapturous. This was a final, wild, fling, the last dice thrown, in her beauty, her power, her feast of vengeance. What would come of it? How would it all end? She scarcely knew: she was aware only of a fierce, unknown force driving her on to fulfil her vow of revenge to the very uttermost. And she was going to defy Basil, the mightiest man she had ever met, hurt Martin whom she loved, and most of all, hurt herself.

At eleven o'clock, when the morning came, she was preparing for one of the most exciting moments in her career; her marriage to Martin. Jacqueline — the trusted little French maid — was in on the secret and accompanying her mistress to witness the affair. Viva was pale and quiet, outwardly, as she let Jacqueline dress her. But inwardly she was strung up to concert-pitch. She dressed very quietly, in a sherry-coloured velvet three-piece; the long coat with deep cuffs and collar of Russian sable. And she wore a little gold cap. Deliberately she avoided wearing any of the jewellery Basil had given her. But she pinned on one shoulder the huge purple bunch of fragrant violets which had come, early that morning, from Martin. She looked exquisite.

Martin awaited her in the little, sunless office, the proudest man in the world on that cold, grey February morning. He, too, was pale with the passionate excitement of it all, but when he saw Viva enter, he flushed darkly red. That a woman so exquisite should condescend to marry him seemed one of the world's miracles. She smiled at him rather strangely, gave him the ring, then her hand. In less than ten minutes the cut-and-dried legal ceremony was over. She was Martin Hayle's wife. His heart pounded as he realised that fact, put an arm around her while she bent over the huge book which the registrar passed to her and in which she was to sign her name.

'My wife —' he whispered passionately, against her ear. Then paused, stared at the name she had written . . . stared at her dumbfounded, wondering if he, or she, were mad.

For she had not signed the register 'Viva Rhodes' as he had anticipated. She had written in her big, loopy handwriting a name which seemed like a ghostly echo of a forgotten past.

'MARY EVEREST.'

'Viva!' said Martin, taking her arm,

'Viva — are you having a joke? You have written Mary Everest's name instead of your own.'

Her heart pounded. She gave a quick, nervous laugh, then handed him the marriage licence.

'Look at that,' she said.

He stared at it and saw that the special licence which she had procured was made out in the names of Martin Hayle and Mary Everest. And then he looked swiftly up at her. His own pulse was jerking fitfully.

'Viva, what does this mean?' he demanded. 'Why have you done this? It isn't legal — to take another woman's name; and in any case, what object have you? Poor Mary Everest is dead and you — '

'She is not dead,' said Viva in a low, strange voice. 'She is living and standing here before you, Martin.'

The registrar, puzzled and embarrassed, looked from bride to bridegroom.

'Pardon me,' he said politely, 'but if there is any error with regard to the names, I suggest — '

'There is no mistake,' interrupted Viva again. 'My name is Mary Everest.'

For a moment, Martin stared at her, wondering if she were labouring under a delusion — or if her brain had suddenly given way. He was distressed and perplexed. He took both her hands and pressed them. Yet the beautiful, perfect face at which he gazed so anxiously was calm, smiling — not the face of one deluded.

'My dear, my darling,' he said, 'think, think quietly. You are Viva Rhodes — not Mary Everest.'

'Martin, aren't you satisfied now I've signed the register?' she asked in the same, strange voice.

'Certainly,' he replied, with a short laugh. 'But we shall have to get married all over again. It won't be legal. You must be married under your own name.'

'It is my name,' she said.

To humour her he quietly accepted the situation and signalled to the registrar, but he was not the thrilled, passionate lover and bridegroom of a few moments ago. He felt deeply distressed and anxious. Why should this beautiful, intelligent Viva behave in this curious fashion — sign the name of her dead friend? But he could not argue or question her here in the registry-office before the other man. So he formally accepted and gave the certificate to Viva, who folded it and placed it in the big Russian leather pochette which she carried. Then they went out to the closed-in car Martin had hired because Viva had not wanted to order it.

Once in the car, driving away from the office, he took her left hand and kissed the new wedding-ring tenderly. But his fine, grey eyes were clouded. It was all so different to his expectations. He could not take her in his arms, call her his 'wife,' feel the thrill and joy of possession. She was not legally his wife, for she had married him under another woman's name.

'Now, my dearest,' he said gravely, 'perhaps you will explain things.'

Her great dark eyes glittered.

'Martin,' she said, 'I *am* Mary Everest.

Viva Rhodes is not my name. It is the name Mr. Rhodes gave me after my operation in Amiens.'

'In Amiens!' he echoed, staring at her.

'Yes, after my accident.'

'What accident?'

'Listen,' she said rapidly. 'I will tell you.'

Martin sat silent, still staring at her in a dumbfounded fashion while she unfolded the story of Mary Everest's departure to Paris; of the accident en route; of the marvellous operations performed upon her mangled face by the great Greek surgeon; of the money he had spent on her in Paris, completing her social education, perfecting her beauty.

'It is true — I swear I am speaking the truth,' she finished breathlessly. 'Look at me, Martin . . . look hard . . . see if you can't recognise Mary . . . in my eyes if nowhere else.'

'Good heavens!' he said hoarsely. 'It is a fairy tale! It can't be true.'

'It is true,' she insisted. 'Look at me.'

He gripped her arms and stared with

new sight at that beautiful, wondrous face that had so enchanted and enthralled him. Not one feature was recognisable. He remembered poor Mary's plain face, but this was the face of a siren, not of a pale, dowdy, unattractive creature like Mary. Yet, on second thoughts, the eyes were the same. His mind leapt back to a certain Christmas Eve when be had seen her gazing at him across the Everest's table . . . those dark, sad eyes . . . yes, they were like the brown eyes of Viva . . . and the hair was the same colour, although cut short now instead of worn in an old-fashioned bun.

'Good heavens!' he said again. He was shaking from head to foot. 'You are doing this to tease me. It can't be true.'

'Don't you remember me, Martin?' She had returned to the old plaintive voice of the Mary of long ago. 'What about that afternoon when we were younger, and you had a motorbike and took Carol and me in the side-car to Richmond? What about the night we all went round to your place and your Aunt Ida tripped over the rug and smashed a coffee-cup and we all laughed at her? What about the day you had us all up at Oxford and Judy spilt the ink in your study all over that pink cotton frock of hers and cried — she was very young then. Oh, I could tell you a dozen things we used to do: the names of your friends at Oxford — Billy Carlyon; Roland Masterton — and how keen you all were about Carol because she was so pretty — and you none of you paid the slightest attention to me because I was so plain . . . '

She paused for breath. Her cheeks were brilliant scarlet with excitement. But Martin was pale, almost ghastly white. He dropped her arms, put a hand to his head. It seemed on fire. For everything she was telling him was true . . . and nobody save Mary could have known those things . . .

'I shall go mad in a minute,' he said. 'But how do I know you aren't laughing at me — that Mary didn't tell you these things in Paris and — ?'

'Mary had no friend in Paris,' said

Viva in a low voice. 'She never reached there. She was smashed up at Amiens — then turned into the Viva you met. If you searched Paris you would never find a grave belonging to her. Mary did not die. Martin, I am Mary! It is no lie. Oh, what more can I do to make you believe it?'

'It is incredible,' he said. 'If it is true — a miracle has been performed.'

'A miracle of plastic surgery — yes.'

'And you owe it all to that Greek, Rhodes.'

'Yes.'

He stared at her again. Then drew a hand across his throbbing brow.

'Good God!' he said. 'It seems impossible — that none of us recognised you. But you are so different from Mary Everest as chalk from cheese.'

'Yes, my own mother might not have recognised me,' she said.

'And you came back to make us all pay,' he said slowly. 'Yes, I am beginning to see things more clearly. You brought Chris Miller to your feet; you came between Carol and me; and now you have married me. It was a glorious revenge.'

'Then you believe that I am Mary?'

He looked down into her dark eyes searchingly.

'I begin to believe it,' he said.

'Nobody will ever know what I suffered,' she said. 'What agonies I endured as the plain, neglected girl — how marvellous it has been to be beautiful and courted.'

'And you have married me for revenge — for vanity?' he said bitterly. 'Good heavens; what a fool I have been!'

Her heart gave a sudden throb of anguish. Her triumph was certainly flat — the taste of victory acid in her mouth. She leaned towards him and placed her hands on his shoulder.

'I have loved you all the way through, Martin,' she said. 'Whatever else I have done you must believe that I love you. I worshipped you, secretly, when I was ugly, and broke my heart that Christmas Eve when you kissed me under the mistletoe . . . then told Carol you had only done it because you were sorry for me.'

He looked at her with doubt and bitterness in his eyes. It seemed to him that he stared at a new being, not at the woman he had adored. This was Mary Everest . . . yes, he remembered that kiss under the mistletoe . . . the expression in her eyes had haunted him for days. And now he could see plainly that they were the same eyes that gazed at him from the beautiful face of the new Mary.

She felt him shake under her hands.

'Oh, Martin, Martin,' she said, 'believe that I love you and have always loved you.'

'How can I believe it?' he said hoarsely. 'You have worked a fine revenge on us all — how can I believe that you have not married me purely for revenge?'

'It isn't true,' she said. 'I married you first because I love you — secondly because I need your protection.'

'From Basil Rhodes?'

'Yes.'

'The man who has given you all the clothes, the money, the Park Lane flat, everything.'

'Yes,' she said, with a shudder. 'And God knows I regret accepting it now. But I was so crazy with joy after my successful operations, I was ready to agree to anything he suggested. Finally I promised to marry him at the end of one year's freedom. But I broke that promise and married you, Martin, because he broke his promise to leave me alone. He has been worrying me, terrifying me; even threatening to destroy the beauty he created.'

Martin breathed hard and fast.

'To destroy the beauty?' he echoed.

'Yes. And I couldn't bear it . . . to be ugly, even repulsive — to lose your love, having once won it; to see you shrink from me . . . Oh, my dear . . . '

Once again she was the enchanting, beautiful woman of his dreams, his desire. She leaned close to him, her breath fragrant on his cheek, her brown eyes swimming with great tears, her

180

lovely mouth quivering. And still he had the wild feeling that she was labouring under a delusion; that she could not be that plain, dowdy Mary, Carol's sister, Judy's sister . . .

'Wouldn't you have married me, if you had known, Martin?' she whispered. 'Does it make all that difference . . . who I am . . . ?'

He suddenly flung his uninjured arm around her. He strained her passionately to his breast and covered her face with burning kisses.

'No, no — nothing matters. I love you and you are mine — my wife,' he cried. 'I don't care whether you are Viva or Mary. To me you will always be Viva — the lovliest woman in the world. I adore you, and you are my wife — my own . . .'

She locked her arms about his neck and responded to his deep, long kisses. And now she was radiant, inexpressibly thrilled, wholly triumphant. For he still loved her — and she was his wife.

'Mine, mine,' he said between the breathless kisses. 'If you love me, nothing else matters.'

'You will forgive me for deceiving you?'

'Yes, yes.'

'For wanting to hurt you — be revenged upon you?' she went on, brokenly.

'Even that, if you truly care for me now.'

'I do — I swear it,' she said.

'Then nothing shall separate us,' he said. 'You shall not go back to that Greek.'

'I meant to go back for a little while,' she panted. 'I'm afraid of him, Martin.'

'He shall not hurt a hair of your head, my beloved. And since he had broken his word to you — threatened you — you owe him nothing.'

'I have begun to hate him,' she said with a shiver.

'You want to come with me, don't you?'

She drew close to him, her arms clinging about his neck.

'Yes, yes, dearest. I don't want to leave

you. I ask nothing in life but to be with you, now.'

Wonderingly he looked down at her.

'Viva . . . Mary . . . whoever you are, you are my wife and my beloved,' he said. 'I adore you.'

'Call me Mary — let me go back to the old Mary; feel that you love her; that it is her you have married,' she said with tears blinding her vision.

'My Mary,' he said, and passionately kissed the tears away. 'Yet it is all so astounding, so extraordinary — it is almost uncanny.'

'I didn't believe it when I first looked at myself in the mirror at the doctor's house in Amiens,' she said.

'What would your family say? They think you are dead.'

'We will tell them the truth,' said Mary. Henceforward she would think of herself as Mary. Viva Rhodes was no more. She was Mary Hayle, Martin's wife. 'Oh, Martin, are you glad that I am beautiful? I am glad . . . because of you . . .'

'Naturally I love your loveliness,' he

said. 'But wonder now that I didn't love you in the old days, my poor, unhappy little Mary.'

'Beauty makes all the difference, Martin,' she said with some bitterness. 'And that is natural.'

All her burning desire for revenge seemed dead within her. All her thirst for conquest, for the destruction of men had also died. She was human, ordinary again — the wife of the man she loved. But there was still Basil Rhodes to deal with, and she was afraid . . .

5

An hour later, Mary sat in her boudoir writing a difficult letter of farewell to Basil Rhodes. Martin was going to The Grange to wait for her to come to him there.

'*If I seem ungrateful in going like this, you have only yourself to blame,*' she wrote. '*You bullied and threatened me and I consider I owe no more allegiance to you. I am Martin Hayle's wife now and wish to live in peace, if you will be big enough, generous enough to leave me alone. For the beauty you gave me and through which I have won the man I have always loved, I shall never cease to thank you, but —*'

Here she paused, pen poised in her slender fingers. Then fear leaped upon her. Her heart gave a terrific jerk — the blood rushed to her temples and receded, leaving her white. She sensed the presence of *somebody* in the little Queen Anne room. She swung round, at the same time gaining her feet. Basil Rhodes stood just behind her. He must have come into the room very softly. She had not even heard him open the door. His was, as usual, a carven face like an ivory mask. But the expression in those light, penetrating eyes of his was frightful. He smiled, however, as he met her terrified gaze.

'Well, *ma mie*!' he said pleasantly. 'So you are married to Martin Hayle. You are leaving me for ever.'

Her dark eyes dilated.

'You — you know that?'

'I know everything. There is nothing Basil Rhodes does not know.'

Then he gripped both her wrists.

'You fool!' he said in a terrible voice. 'You little fool to defy me. Did I not tell you that if you broke your promise to marry me I should destroy you?'

'Let me go,' she panted. 'You have no right to say such things. Let me go, I say . . .'

'Fool!' he said again. 'Fools, both of you. I could not stop the marriage — I did not know in time — but when Masri came back from Marylebone and told me what had happened I vowed you should pay for it, and you shall — you shall, *ma chère*!'

She licked dry lips, tried to free her wrists. A greater terror than she had ever known seized her in this hour.

'Basil, let me go — you have no right to stop me!' she gasped. 'I am Martin's wife now; you can't hurt me. If you touch me, he'll — he'll kill you.'

'I shall kill him first,' said the Greek with a low laugh. 'If he comes near me, he shall pay as you are going to pay. I made you, created you; I named you Viva, and claimed you for my own. You have chosen to defy me, to be Mary Everest again — even to marry that English fool. Very well, your punishment shall be as great as your glory has been.'

She began to struggle, to scream in a frenzied fashion. She was stiff with fear, because she did not know what he meant to do.

'You can scream,' he said. 'Only Masri

and the Indians can hear you, and they will all three serve me. You played excellently into my hands, *ma chère*, when you sent your maid off before you. As for Irene, she will neither know nor care what becomes of you. She hates you — she has a wife from Greece in view for me.'

'Basil! Basil!' the girl moaned and gasped his name, bruising her delicate wrists in the wild endeavour to loosen his steely grip. 'Don't hurt me — you loved me once — '

A curious look of grief, of agony, of hatred combined convulsed the Greek's handsome features. He seized her left hand, tore off the wedding-ring, flung it away.

'I made you — you were mine — my Viva!' he muttered.

She believed that he was mad — that she was dealing with a genius whose brain was crazed. She fell on her knees before him, sick with fright.

'Basil — let me go!' she stammered.

But suddenly he whipped something out of his pocket. She could not see what it was at first, but when she felt a sudden sharp prick on her left arm, she shrieked aloud. She knew what it was — a hypodermic needle. What had he given her? What devilish drug? Was it death?

'Martin . . .' She moaned her husband's name just before she felt the dark mists descend upon her and drifted into unconsciousness.

Basil Rhodes felt the slim figure of the girl go limp in his arms. For an instant he stared down at her. Then an evil triumphant look came into his light grey eyes.

'Little fool!' he whispered. 'You think you are Mary Hayle, but you are still Viva Rhodes . . . mine . . . mine!'

He laid her down on a couch at the other end of the room. Then he rang the bell for Masri.

'Order the saloon and tell the Indians to get ready to accompany their mistress and me. You come too. We leave London at once,' he said.

The Arab boy glanced at the still figure on the sofa, with indifference in his liquid brown eyes, then made a deep obeisance to his master. He was utterly Basil Rhodes' slave — had been since the day, a year ago, when the Greek had picked him out of the gutter in the slums of Cairo where he had been starving, and made use of his beautiful face and crafty young brain.

Then Basil sat down at the Queen Anne bureau at which poor Mary had been sitting half an hour ago. Carefully he studied the half-written note. Then he took another sheet of notepaper and began to write to Martin Hayle.

When Martin — every inch the thrilled and happy bridegroom — reached The Grange, he found the Everests at lunch. They were there, Mr. Everest, Judy, Carol, Jack. Carol greeted Martin somewhat stiffly.

'You're looking as though you'd come into money,' she sniffed. 'Beaming all over.'

'Am I?' He gave a boyish laugh and refused the chair the maid brought forward for him. He commenced to pace up and down the little oak-furnished dining-room, quickly, excitedly. 'Well, I have two very astounding pieces of news for you all. One so astonishing that I doubt if you will believe it.'

'Gracious!' said Judy, dropping her pudding-spoon. 'Whatever is it, Martin?'

'First of all I am married,' he said.

A wave of red rushed across Carol's face. She pushed an untidy lock of golden hair back from her forehead with a characteristic gesture. Her lips were hard and sullen.

'Oh!' she exclaimed.

'Indeed, my boy,' said Mr. Everest. 'And to whom?'

'To the girl you know as Viva Rhodes.'

'Of course,' muttered Judy. 'That woman . . .'

'Jolly good for you!' said Jack Everest. 'She's a cinch.'

'Oh you shut up!' said his sisters in angry chorus.

Martin looked round the family, his eyes brilliant.

'Do you know who 'that woman' is?' he asked.

'Now you come to ask, nobody does seem to know,' said old Mr. Everest. 'Half-Greek, isn't she? Dear, dear, Martin, my boy, does your father approve of this hasty marriage?'

'He doesn't know. We were only married an hour ago.'

'Then where is Viva?' asked Judy.

'Packing and then coming straight here.'

'Why here?' said Carol, tossing her head. 'I should think this would be the last place you'd bring her, Martin.'

He flushed slightly.

'Wait till you know, Carol,' he said. 'Then you will forgive what appears to you my bad taste.'

'Know what,' demanded Carol.

Martin paused before her, hand in his pocket.

'Does it — has it ever occurred to you that Viva Rhodes bears any resemblance to Mary?' he asked.

'To Mary!' echoed Carol. 'Heavens, no!'

'Fancy asking that,' said Judy. 'Poor

old Mary wasn't a bit like Viva.'

'What about the eyes — the colour of the hair?'

'Oh, they both had dark brown eyes, yes — and perhaps the same coloured hair,' admitted Carol. 'But Viva Rhodes is beautiful and Mary was not. But what are you driving at, Martin?'

'This,' he said, excitedly. 'She is Mary.'

'Who is?'

'The girl you know as Viva Rhodes and who is now my wife.'

Silence. The Everests all ceased eating. All eyes were focussed upon Martin. Then old Mr. Everest cleared his throat.

'My dear lad!' he protested. 'Is this a joke?'

'No, I thought it was one when Viva signed the register Mary Everest,' said Martin. 'But it proved to be no joke. She is Mary, your daughter.'

'Martin, you're mad!' said Carol shrilly. 'Mary is dead.'

'Mary did not die,' said Martin. 'Nor did she ever have a friend, Viva Rhodes. She *became* Viva Rhodes.'

The Everests exchanged glances. Then Jack gave a nervous laugh.

'I say, you're mad, Martin,' he said.

'Listen — I will tell you about it,' said Martin more quietly. He sat down and related to them, word for word, the strange dramatic story that Mary had unfolded to him. They listened with eyes staring, mouths agape, excited, incredulous, believing, in turns. It all seemed impossible — a fairy story — a melodrama. They heard of the accident at Amiens; of the wonderful surgery performed by Dr. Rhodes; of Mary's beauty; of her education in Paris, then of her desire to return to the old home disguised and be revenged upon all those who had mocked and neglected her.

'At first I could not believe it,' Martin said. 'But gradually it struck me as all being very true. I could see Mary in remarks only she could have made. She remembered lots of intimate things we had done years ago — the names of my Oxford pals — of places we'd been to — a dozen things that happened.'

'Good heavens!' said Mr. Everest.

He had risen, his table-napkin fell to the ground, his rubicund face was pale. He mopped his forehead with a large handkerchief.

'Good heavens!' he said again. 'Is it possible? That girl — our Mary!'

Carol and Judy were quite white. They both had that peculiar, sick feeling of the uncanny which Martin had had when first Mary had told him her story.

'Viva Rhodes — Mary!' gasped Judy.

'Oh, I can't believe it!' cried Carol. 'How could any surgeon have altered her face so completely?'

'It was done in the war,' muttered Jack.

'Besides, how could she have known so much of my past history — or yours?' said Martin. 'No amount of schooling from Mary to her supposed friend could have brought that about. I asked her the most difficult questions and she never faltered, never made a slip. She was Mary; she spoke like Mary; her eyes were Mary's, only her features were different.'

'Now I come to think of it, her eyes are

exactly the same,' said Judy in a hushed voice. 'And her height, her build, her feet. I remember we used to say Mary was ugly, but she had the prettiest ankles in the family — and that glossy brown hair — yes — I begin to believe it's true.'

'Jove!' ejaculated Jack. 'It's incredible!'

Carol was flushed and breathing hard.

'Mary!' she muttered. 'Mary come back to life . . . and she never did die in Paris; all that was eyewash.'

'But why, why did she do it? Why behave in such an extraordinary way?' asked Mr. Everest.

'Because, poor girl, she was crazy with bitterness, with the longing to get back at us all for neglecting her,' said Martin sombrely.

'Well, she's behaved pretty badly,' said Carol. 'She took Chris from Judy and now she's married you.'

'So you're my son-in-law after all!' said Mr. Everest excitedly. 'And I've got my Mary back. Dear, dear, dear, what a miracle! What a wonderful era we live in! I'm quite longing to see my girl again — to make sure.'

'I shall not be certain she's Mary until I've asked her a few questions,' said Carol.

'Nor will I, if it comes to that,' muttered Judy. Then she added with a short laugh, 'What will Chris say?'

'Yes, what will he say?' echoed Carol. 'Mary used to bore him to tears. Heavens! How she's changed if she really is Mary.'

'I'm certain that she is,' said Martin.

'I can make sure,' said Mr. Everest. 'Perhaps you girls have forgotten that when Mary was two years old, she was scalded on the left leg with boiling water dropped on her by a careless nursemaid — the girl, Dolly, we used to have.'

'I remember,' said Carol. 'Judy and Jack wouldn't, they're too young.'

'Well, it left a permanent scar,' said Mr. Everest. Martin nodded, his handsome eyes still brilliant.

'She spoke of that,' he said. 'And no doubt she can show you the scar.'

'I'm beginning to feel terribly excited,'

said Judy. 'I wish she'd come.'

'There goes the bell!' exclaimed Jack.

The entire Everest family rushed to the door. They had forgotten their suspicions, their resentment, toward the 'Greek' woman, Viva Rhodes. They wanted to see Mary — their Mary. Blood-ties are strong, and after all, Mary had been one of them. Her death had seemed unimportant, but her miraculous return seemed the most important thing in the world — because she had grown beautiful and wonderful — and she was Martin Hayle's wife.

But it was the French maid, Jacqueline, who stood on the doorstep.

'I have brought ze luggage,' she said smiling. 'My Madame is coming on in a mineet.'

They returned to the drawing-room. They were all seething with excitement now, with longing to see and question this girl who claimed to be Mary. The moments dragged by like hours . . .

They waited two hours and still Mary did not come. Jacqueline expressed surprise.

'Madame was all ready. I do not un'er-stand,' she said, shrugging her shoulders.

Martin suddenly grew afraid.

'I ought to have insisted on staying with her,' he said. 'I don't trust that Greek fellow, and I know she fears him.'

'Might he do something awful because she promised to marry him?' breathed Judy.

Martin frowned.

'He is not supposed to be there.'

'*Mais non!* Monsieur went away for the day to a hospital,' said Jacqueline. 'Madame was alone.'

Another hour dragged by. When four o'clock struck, the Everests were disappointed and doubtful, and Martin lost patience.

'I am going round to Park Lane,' he said. 'I must find out what has happened.'

'Let us all go,' suggested Carol. 'If she is really Mary, we might as well go with you.'

'I'll stay here,' said Mr. Everest. 'Bring her back, you children. I daren't come with you. The excitement is bad for my heart.'

Martin, Carol, Judy, Jacqueline and Jack boarded a taxi and drove to Park Lane. Martin was anxious now. He reproached himself a dozen times over for not having accompanied his young wife — for letting her go alone to the flat. Supposing something had happened to her . . . his love . . . his own wife . . . ?

He grew even more apprehensive and worried when the door of Rhodes' flat was opened to the little group by a servant whom he did not recognise. The man who answered the bell was a French chef, generally in the kitchen. He seemed in a bad temper, but answered Martin's questions.

'Madame is not here.'

Martin's heart gave a sick throb.

'Not here? Then where is she?'

'I do not know, M'sieu. I only know she and M'sieu left here two hours ago with the Indians and the boy, Masri. I was told to go and find fresh servants for M'sieu's sister, who comes back to-night.

I am very busy.'

'But what do you mean — that Madame left here with M'sieu?' demanded Martin.

'What I saw,' said the Frenchman, shrugging his shoulders. 'With M'sieu Rhodes. I did not see them go, but he came and told me they were just going.'

Martin staggered back. Mary . . . Viva . . . whoever she was, gone . . . with Basil Rhodes . . . ! It could not be true.

'Is there no message for me?' he asked the man hoarsely. 'My name is Hayle.'

'Ah! There is a note for you which Madame wrote,' said the man and shuffled away. He returned with a sealed envelope.

Martin took it, stared at the handwriting with incredulous eyes. He knew that it was from the woman he loved and had married. She had written to him before and this was her handwriting.

'*Revenge is sweet, Martin,*' the letter began. '*Now I am satisfied. I brought you all to my feet. I am your wife, but I shall never live with you. I am returning to the Continent with Basil Rhodes. I can laugh at you all.*

Viva Rhodes — *otherwise* Mary Everest.

Martin read this extraordinary, unexpected note twice. Then a red mist seemed to come across his eyes. His heart beat with slow, painful throbs. The face he turned to the Everests was ghastly.

'My God!' he muttered.

'What is it? Where is she?' asked Carol.

'Gone,' said Martin in a hollow tone. 'She has just done this to complete her revenge. She has fooled us all.'

'No, no,' said the faithful Jacqueline. 'It isn't true — of that I am sure. My lady has been kidnapped — something has happened — but she has not gone of her own accord.'

Martin turned to her, his heart pounding.

'What do you mean? Why do you say that?'

'Because I am sure of it, M'sieu. She sent me on to you wiz ze luggage. She say,

'Oh, Jacqueline, I love M'sieu so much, I am going to leave everything for him, but first I must write to *M'sieu le Docteur* and say good-bye.' The tears were in her so beautiful eyes when she spoke of you, M'sieu — I am certain she adore you.'

The colour returned to Martin's cheeks. He stared from the excited little French maid to Carol and Judy who were watching them curiously.

'God knows what I believe,' he muttered. 'There is this letter — '

'It isn't Mary's handwriting,' said Carol.

'But it's the writing of Viva Rhodes,' said Judy.

'She may have cultivated that,' said Martin.

'Or it may perhaps have been written bly *M'sieu le Docteur*,' put in Jacqueline sagely.

'You mean forged?' said Martin swiftly.

'Oui, M'sieu. I am positive Ma'mselle would never have written that to you whom she adore. She meant to come wiz me — to you. I know it.'

Martin put a hand to his swimming head. The servant had shut the front door of the Rhodes' flat in his face. They were grouped there outside in the hall. He tried to gather his scattered thoughts — to decide whether Viva, Mary, whoever she was . . . had deliberately fooled and left him, or been taken forcibly away by the Greek.

He felt suddenly ashamed of his lack of faith compared with Jacqueline's belief in her mistress. The Frenchwoman was more loyal, more loving than he — who professed to love her!

'Heaven forgive me, I don't know what to think,' he groaned.

Then he began to remember little things Mary had said to him about Basil Rhodes; tales of his great power and strength, both physical and mental; her fear of him; yes, she had been afraid — he was sure of it — afraid even while she stole away to marry him. He recalled his last meeting with her; their drive in the car after their marriage; her strange confession that she was Mary

Everest — made Mary Hayle by the marriage-bond. How she had broken down and cried against his heart; told of her dread, her dislike of the Greek; how he had kissed and comforted and sworn to protect her.

'I am rotten — a weak, poor lover — to fall into the first trap the Greek has set for me,' he reflected. 'No doubt Jacqueline is right. Mary has been spirited away by that fellow against her will; and I am doubting, condemning her without making the slightest effort to protect or help her.'

His lips shut in a grim line. He swung round to Mary's two sisters, who seemed speechless with mystification.

'Jacqueline is right,' he cried. 'Mary has been taken away against her will. I am sure Jacqueline is right — that she would have come to me if she could.

'Yes, yes, M'sieu — she adore you — and she is mortally afraid of *M'sieu le Docteur!*' said the maid, bursting into sobs.

'Don't cry,' said Martin. 'I shall do

everything in my power to find her.'

'It sounds strange to hear you call her 'Mary',' muttered Carol. 'Can that part of it be true, I wonder?'

A sudden brain-wave led Martin to say:

'When she signed her name in the register, she signed it Mary Everest — no doubt in her old, familiar handwriting. We will drive to Marylebone and you shall look at her signature, you and Judy. See if you recognise it. Come — at once!'

They drove away from Park Lane to the registry-office. There Carol and Judy examined the book, wherein Mary had written her maiden name.

'It's Mary's handwriting!' said Carol.

'Yes, it is — without any doubt. That Greek 'e' at the end and that sprawling 'M'; it's Mary's hand!' said Judy.

'I remember it too,' said Martin sombrely.

'Then Viva really is our sister,' said Carol in a voice of awe.

'And my wife,' added Martin.

They walked into the street again.

Martin felt sick with fear of the unknown.

'But what has happened to her?' he groaned.

'It is *M'sieu le Docteur* who has taken her away,' wept Jacqueline. 'He is cruel; I am sure of it!'

'We must find her,' said Carol.

Martin's hand reached out and sought hers.

'Carol,' he said huskily, 'I treated you badly — let you down; but will you forgive me and help me to find her? I'm a kind of brother to you now.'

The girl flushed and pressed his hand.

'Yes, all right, Martin,' she said generously. 'I'll help you. Heaven knows I don't want any harm to come to Mary.'

'Nor do I,' seconded Judy. 'But I must get hold of Chris and tell him about things. He was pretty smitten with her' — she gave a short laugh — 'but when he learns who she is and that she's Mrs. Hayle now, he may give us a hand.'

'Let's all go back to The Grange and ring up Chris,' suggested Carol.

The little party drove back to Dene

Park.

When Chris Miller arrived and was told the uncanny story of Viva's real origin, he was, needless to say, as flabbergasted and incredulous as the rest had been. But after being told the various proofs, he was forced to believe that the beautiful, amusing, fascinating girl at whose feet he had flung himself, was old Mary Everest.'

'It's astounding!' he said, flushed and unnerved, staring from one face to another. 'Yet now one thinks of it, she *is* a beautiful replica of Mary. Those brown eyes, and that hair, and figure.'

'And now this Greek fiend has taken her away,' said Martin between his teeth. 'And she is my wife. Do you realise that Chris?'

'I'm trying to,' said Chris with a nervous laugh. 'And if it's a fact I'll help you look for her. I gave her my promise that I'd be her friend, and I won't break it.'

'It's all like a bit out of a film or a book,' said Judy.

Chris turned to her. His blue eyes

looked a trifle guilty.

'I've been rotten to you, Judy,' he said in a low tone. 'It was a sort of madness; but I'm not mad now. I only want to help Martin: to find her because she's his wife and — your sister.'

Judy suddenly choked and turned from him. He followed her, put an arm round her.

'Try and forgive me,' he whispered.

'That's all right, Chris,' she said, wiping her eyes fiercely. 'Don't let's talk about that part of it, though. She's our Mary come back to life, and Martin's wife.'

'You're all being wonderful about it,' said Martin, with suspiciously bright eyes. 'Thank you awfully — all of you. After all it was our past treatment of her that turned her into what she was as Viva Rhodes. And now she's just Mary Hayle, my wife; it's up to us to find her, to rescue her from that fiend, Dr. Rhodes. But how the deuce shall we set about it?'

'A detective,' suggested Chris.

'Yes. We'll ring up Scotland Yard at

once.'

'Then there's the doctor's sister, Miss Rhodes, who is still at Park Lane. We must see her, question her.'

'Yes,' nodded Martin. 'We'll do that. Let's get on to the Yard first.'

'And don't spare expense,' put in old Mr. Everest. 'If it's Mary, my daughter, I'm going to have a financial finger in the pie and find her along with the rest of you.'

Which all goes to prove that despite petty jealousies and likes and dislikes and differences of opinion, family ties are strong, and blood is thicker than water.

★   ★   ★

Meanwhile, what of Mary?

She knew nothing of what was happening to her for hours after the struggle with Basil and the injection which had been forcibly given her. She was unconscious, in a heavy, drugged sleep, powerless to protest or resist anybody or anything.

It had been simple enough for the

cunning Greek to get her away from the flat without attracting attention from inmates of neighbouring flats, or passers-by in the streets. He just rolled her up in a Persian rug which the two Indians carried down into the waiting car, then drove away with the Indians and the Arab boy. To an onlooker, a beautiful rug was being taken away from the flat, nothing more.

Once out of London, on the outskirts of the town, the rug was unrolled and Mary Hayle was allowed fresh air. She lay motionless in the closed car with Basil's arm around her, her beautiful bare head lolling against his shoulder, her face ghastly pale. Every now and then the doctor tested her pulse and looked at the whites of her eyes. He made sure she was not suffering unduly from the drug.

Once or twice he lifted one of her inert, slim hands and kissed it passionately.

'My Viva — the Viva of my creation — not the wife of that English pup,' he muttered to himself in his own language. 'You shall see . . . you shall see who is master.'

She slept on in that drugged sleep, insensible to his touch or voice. Dark, fantastic dreams chased through her stupefied brain; haunting, weird, terrifying phantoms of the drug that mastered her. Now and then she stirred, moaned as though in pain or fright. And then the Greek doctor watched her curiously, with a cold, frozen interest in his victim.

The great, powerful touring-car reached the outskirts of an Essex village and swept through to lonely countryland, flat and desolate in the winter dusk. Basil Rhodes owned a house in Essex: a great stone mansion in the centre of a huge dilapidated garden. Once it had been a prosperous estate. Long since the owners had died, and the big place was left to rot and crumble, until the Greek saw it, in passing through the village of Ashgretting, and bought it up for a mere song. It was remote, off the main road, out of common observation, and he felt certain it would one day be useful. To this gloomy house he now conveyed the girl whose beauty he had created and whose soul he wished to destroy.

Masri the Arab, accompanied by the two Indians, was sent into the village to buy provisions and candles, for there was no gas or electric light, and a room was prepared for Mary. Rhodes had bought the place as it had stood, half furnished with heavy, rotting Victorian furniture and faded, moth-eaten draperies.

The scene upon which the unfortunate girl finally opened her eyes was distinctly terrifying. She found herself lying on an immense four-poster bed, covered with a dilapidated quilt. For the moment her brain, her eyes, were too dazed to take in her surroundings. Her temples throbbed with pain and she felt sick after the strong drug administered to her. But gradually she grew capable of taking in her surroundings.

First she saw Basil sitting beside her, his handsome, cruel face turned from her. He was calmly smoking a cigar, lolling back in his chair, apparently deep in thought. She remembered with a violent jerk of the pulse what had taken place in London in her flat — she had fought with Basil and he had drugged her. Where had he brought her? What would Martin say when she failed to turn up at The Grange?

She stared about her, her eyes dilating, and saw the manner of room wherein she lay. It was icy-cold and gloomy beyond description. Torn, ancient red curtains were drawn across a big bay window. There was no carpet on the bare boards, only odd pieces of brown paper. It was thick with dust and smelt disagreeably — that musty odour a room takes on when it has long been kept from fresh air. On a gaunt-looking mahogany dressing-chest stood two wax candles in chipped enamel sticks. These candles threw dim, flickering yellow light up to the ceiling, the plaster of which was torn and cracked. The light was so dim that it served only to enhance the horror of the big desolate room; to cast phantom shadows on the walls and make the darkness of the corners more dense.

After Mary's beautiful golden bedroom in Park Lane, the light, the luxury, the perfumed sweetness of her home, this strange bedroom struck dread and chill at her heart. She struggled into a sitting posture and pushed her disordered hair back from her brow.

'Where am I? What has happened?' she gasped.

'Ah, awake are you?' said Basil Rhodes softly. And he put down his cigar and stood up, stared down at her with a knife-edged smile. She looked wildly up at him.

'Why have you brought me here? What is this horrible place?' she panted.

'One of my minor possessions,' he said, shrugging his massive shoulders. 'A little, forsaken mansion in Ashgretting, Essex, about fifty miles out of London. The name is Ashgretting Hall, and it has not been lived in for twenty years.'

Mary stared about her again. Now, with sharper vision, she could take in the frightful desolation and ruin of the place. Everything seemed in the last stages of decay. Filthy cobwebs hung from an enormous chandelier in the centre of the ceiling, and even as she sat there, staring, a mouse scuttled boldly across the floor.

Mary gave a low cry and gained her feet, stood there swaying, a hand clasped to her forehead.

'Oh, take me away from this — this *grave*!' she gasped. 'Basil, you are mad to have brought me here.'

'You were mad to defy me,' he said. 'If this place displeases you, *ma mie*, you have only to do as I ask and you can be conveyed by my car back to your Park Lane flat — at once.'

She shrank away from him.

'Do what you ask?' She gave a short, nervous laugh. 'And what might that be?'

'Write a letter to M'sieu Martin Hayle at once telling him to annul your marriage because you are living with me and intend to marry me.'

She flushed crimson.

'Never! I shall die before you ever make me live with you — marry you — you fiend!'

His pale, magnetic eyes narrowed to pin-pricks.

'Very well, *ma chère*,' he said lightly. 'Then you must remain here.'

'I — I am Martin's wife!' she said bravely. 'He will find me.'

'Oh no — never. He will never dream of looking for you here. Besides, I have already sent him a note in that charming handwriting of yours, telling him that you have deliberately run away with me back to France . . . to complete your revenge.'

A look of despair crossed Mary's face.

'You have done that? Oh, my God!'

'Yes. So he will not even trouble to look for you. He will realise he was duped by you — made a tool of revenge. But I do not intend you to bear his name. You belong to me. It is I whose wife you shall be. You are Viva Rhodes; never Mary Everest again.'

She sat down on the edge of the bed. Her beautiful dark eyes were wide with dread and despair. She knew only too well the colossal willpower and cunning of this Greek. He would stop at nothing to gain his own ends. And Martin might indeed believe in that forged letter — put her right out of his life; never trouble to search for her.

'Martin, my love!' she inwardly groaned, and hid her face in her hands.

Then suddenly she looked up at the man who was for the moment her master.

'Basil — you said you loved me once,' she said in a hollow tone. 'Is this how you prove it?'

'My love is not of the unselfish kind, I admit,' he said, with a cold smile. 'I do not intend to give you up to Hayle. I made that perfect face of yours, and either you shall belong to me, or I shall carry out my threat to destroy the beauty; and then, maimed and hideous, you shall be returned to — your husband!'

The callous, devilish words, filled Mary with sick horror. The man was diabolical, she thought, inhuman. But he did not merely threaten. Of that she was sure. So she would be called upon to choose between beauty and power as the wife of Basil Rhodes; or a seamed, wrecked face for life — and Martin. Ah, but not Martin. She could never go back to him thus — never bear to see him wince at the sight of that face he had worshipped made a travesty.

'Oh, you are cruel — fiendish!' she said with a sob. 'But I won't give in to you. I won't!'

He caught her in his arms, held her like a vice.

'You madden me; you make me feel like giving you your punishment to-night,' he muttered. 'To slash that insolent, beautiful face of yours with my knife; then let you go to your husband.'

She shuddered. She was sick with fear. She believed that she was in the hands of a madman. The light of insanity burned in the Greek's eyes. But her dark eyes held his courageously, without flinching, and suddenly he laughed and let her go.

'No — it would be a pity,' he said. 'You are as lovely, as desirable as the moon-goddess, as the passion-flower, my Viva. I will break that stubborn spirit of yours before I destroy your beauty. You will give in — forget Martin Hayle before I have finished with you.'

Her teeth chattered.

'What do you mean to do?'

'You shall see,' he said. 'And let me tell you, *ma mie*, to spare your breath should you desire to scream for help. Ashgretting Hall is one mile from the village, surrounded by trees, quite out of sight and sound. Nobody would hear you or help you. My Indians and my Arab are the only other inmates of this place besides myself, and they are my loyal servants. Now I will leave you to think things over. As soon as you come to the wise conclusion that you will cut Martin Hayle out of your life and marry me, just ring that bell over your bed. It works, fortunately. I wish you a pleasant night's rest.'

'Wait, wait!' she cried, as he started to walk towards the door. 'Are — are you staying in this horrible house, too?'

'I leave you to guess that,' he replied

with the cold, fiendish smile such as the torturers of the Spanish Inquisition must have worn. '*Adieu, ma mie!*'

Then he was gone. The rusty key turned in the lock. Mary was a prisoner.

She immediately rushed to the window, parted the curtains and peered out. No hope of escape here. Basil had placed her in a back bedroom at the top of the house which must have once been a nursery, for the window was barred with iron from top to bottom. The darkness veiled the garden from her. But she could see vague shapes of leafless trees, great gaunt branches waving in the wind, and it was raining: the drops spattered against the dirt-encrusted panes.

With a feeling of utter despair, she turned back to the room, so hideous, so full of flickering shadows and strange shapes, enough to frighten a woman with a stronger nerve than hers. She was tired in body and brain, and felt ill from the effect of the drug.

Whether or not the inhuman doctor meant to starve her, she neither knew nor cared. She only thought of Martin and what he would think. She flung herself down on the bed and buried her face on her arm. Great sobs racked her slender body. The scalding tears streamed down her cheeks.

'Martin, my love, my darling,' she sobbed. 'I mean to be true to you, whatever that fiend does to me!'

* * *

Miss Irene Rhodes was interviewed and cross-questioned by both Martin Hayle and Chris Miller. She listened to what the two young Englishmen had to say with faint curiosity. She was well aware of what had happened to Mary and where Basil had taken the girl. Basil had left a note for her, explaining his actions. But she did not know that Mary had told Martin her real identity and married him. That interested her.

It must be remembered that Irene had never liked the girl her brother had saved from the wreck at Amiens and modelled into a dream of beauty, neither had she approved of his desired marriage with Mary. She was a proud, cold, haughty woman without any of Basil's hot impulses and passionate whims. She disapproved strongly of many of his methods, particularly of his mad wish to marry a girl who obviously did not wish to become his wife.

She considered it Basil's duty to his fine old Grecian name and ancestors to marry a girl from Greece — a woman of as proud and old a lineage as he, himself. This Mary Everest was nothing; nobody; beautiful only because he had made her so, distinguished only because he had given her the veneer.

Coolly and with some contempt she sat listening to Martin Hayle's heated discourse upon the 'lovely, innocent girl Dr. Rhodes had abducted,' etc., etc. Finally she said in a tone of ice:

'You are anxious to rescue your — er — wife from my brother. Well, I am anxious to rescue him from her. She is not the wife I would have chosen. From boyhood Basil has been foolishly head-strong and unprincipled. As a rule I have never interfered with him. But now — '

'Well, now?' said Martin eagerly. 'Don't you think it your duty to help us find Mary, Miss Rhodes?'

Martin and Chris knew beyond all doubt now that the beautiful dark-eyed Viva was Mary. Miss Rhodes had admitted that, told them how Mary had been brought to the Amiens hospital a mangled, disfigured wreck, and how Basil had performed the miraculous operations upon her face.

Miss Rhodes considered the case for a moment. She was not frightened of her brother: the one person in the world who was mentally his superior, and the stronger character of the two; Basil might fume and rant if she gave away his hiding place, but he could not touch her. And once this common, silly English girl was returned to her relations, he would soon forget her, and go back to France to work.

'I will tell you where to find the girl,'

she said indifferently. Martin leapt to his feet. His haggard young face flushed. Chris stood beside him, tingling.

An hour later four men were driving at breakneck speed to Essex, in a fast car. They were Martin, Chris, a man in plain clothes from Scotland Yard, and a policeman, also in plain clothes. Martin was taking no risks. He felt certain there would be a fight; that the Greek would not give Mary up without some sort of struggle, and he intended to go armed and with help.

It was late afternoon when the car turned into Ashgretting village. They stopped at the Boar's Head Inn, and made enquiries about Ashgretting Hall. They were at first told that the place had been deserted and unoccupied for years; then a village wag informed them that lights had been seen in the rooms at the Hall.

The detective advised Martin to leave the car at the inn and go on foot to Ashgretting Hall.

'If you think this fellow is going to put

up a fight, we'd far better attack warily,' he said.

Martin agreed. It was a dark moonless evening and a thick vapourish mist hung over the flat Essex countryside. The weather certainly aided them. They could creep up the drive of Ashgretting Hall, unseen from any window.

Martin's pulse thrilled and his heart pounded as the little party approached the house wherein he believed his young wife was a prisoner. His anxiety was intense.

'My darling, my darling, what has happened to you?' he thought, strained with fear for her. 'If that Greek brute has so much as touched your hand, I shall want to kill him!'

The four men paused when they reached the Hall. Not a person was in sight; not a sound broke the stillness of the night. They had walked on the grass, fearing to tread on the gravel drive and rouse attention by the scrunching. They walked all round the house and then Martin pointed to an upper room at the back, over the porch.

'There's a light up there, behind red curtains,' he whispered to the detective. 'Shall I climb up there and try to look in?'

'You can't, sir, with your arm in a sling. Let me,' said the man.

'No, I will,' said Chris.

It was Chris who, with youthful agility, swung himself up by the thick, strong ivy that trailed over the house, balanced himself on the porch, then managed to get a view into the lighted room. Fortune favoured him, for although the window was barred, it was half open and he could hear voices inside; he could also see through a gap in the tattered curtains. One had been ripped down by Mary in the night and only put back very carelessly.

The Greek was not prepared for invasion; had not dreamed that his sister's dislike of Mary would lead her to betray him.

What Chris saw and heard made his face whiten and his blood boil within him.

'My God — what a beast!' he muttered.

Mary had lain on the four-poster bed, sick and weak and in despair, most of the day. Hour after hour Basil had approached her, alternately pleading and threatening, trying to force her to surrender, to fly with him to Paris. And she had resisted, refused, clung to her love for Martin.

Now he was using more drastic measures — had hit upon a fiendish plan for forcing her into surrender. Chris saw her sitting on the edge of the bed, brown hair dishevelled, her beautiful face a mask of suffering and horror. The Greek was standing by her.

'Yes, we have your fine husband in the house,' he was saying in a low, cruel voice. 'My Indians got him down here as easily as you were brought. He is in the next room.'

'Martin — Martin here?' asked Mary in a voice that wrung Chris's heart. 'Oh, let me go to him, Basil.'

'Oh, no!' said the Greek. 'You are going to say good-bye to him for ever and marry me.'

'Never, never.'

'Very well — he shall suffer for it,' said Rhodes. 'He is in the hands of my Indians now. They are very excellent fellows — and they excel particularly in the art of torture.'

'What do you mean?' she gasped.

'I mean that they will torture him,' the Greek spat at her. 'Until you surrender.'

'I don't believe it; you are only fooling me!' Mary panted, hands pressed to her galloping heart.

Rhodes gave a fiendish smile.

'Listen,' he said. Then gave a peculiar whistle which obviously was a signal.

The next moment a terrible moan was heard; a muffled, hoarse scream; a cry that suggested horrible agony. And it was followed by a man's moaning cry.

The girl on the bed sprang to her feet and clutched at the doctor's arm.

'It is Martin. What are they doing to him? Martin — Martin!' she screamed frenziedly, thoroughly taken in by the clever acting.

'Well, are you going to give in now?' asked the Greek.

Chris waited to hear no more. With furious, indignant eyes and a face suffused with colour he slid down the ivy and gained Martin's side.

'The devil — the fiend incarnate!' he gasped. 'Martin, do you know what they are doing?'

He told them rapidly what he had seen and heard. And Martin was white to the lips when he understood. Mary was true to him, loyal to her love, and Rhodes was pretending that her husband was a prisoner; was pretending that he, Martin, was being put to torture. He pictured her horror and anguish. He knew that whereas she could be strong on all other points she would break down now, give way to the Greek's demands rather than let him suffer.

'My brave darling,' he thought exultantly. Then he said:

'Now boys, into that house, and if it's

a fight, then we'll fight to the end — for her!'

The next moment they had opened the window on the ground floor and jumped through, one after the other. Masri was upstairs, in the room adjoining Mary's. It was he, cunning little actor, who was mimicking Martin's voice, uttering those blood-curdling groans. The Indians were in a room in the other wing of the house playing some native game, engrossed in their sport.

Basil Rhodes was a surprised man when the door of the bedroom was flung open and four armed men rushed in. He had been on the brink of victory. Mary had just flung herself at his feet and told him she would marry him, do anything rather than let Martin be tortured any more.

The girl, half-dazed with the frightful strain through which she had been put, was still crouching on the floor when the four men entered the room. Through a kind of a haze she saw Martin — not a white tortured prisoner, but a flushed, passionately angry man eager to rescue and avenge her. She gave a cry and struggled to her feet.

'Martin! — Martin!' she moaned.

He caught her in his arms and lifted her right off the ground, forgetting the pain in his arm which was not yet quite healed.

'Mary, my poor, poor darling!' he said.

She fainted with the sheer relief and joy of it even as she felt his passionate adoring kisses on her mouth.

Basil Rhodes stood motionless between the two men from Scotland Yard. Chris was cursing him in round, British fashion for his brutality. The Greek's carven face was frozen into a mask, his light grey eyes like rapiers. He smiled very coldly at the heated boy, then looked across the room to where stood Martin with his wife in his arms.

'So you win!' he said at length. 'And now you would put me in prison for abduction, eh? But no, that would never do. Basil Rhodes shall never suffer imprisonment — never be utterly defeated. Without my Mary, what have I to live for?'

'Take care!' said Martin sharply.

But he was too late. The doctor's hand had gone swiftly to his lips, carried to them a swift, subtle poison which he carried in a signet-ring, and the next moment he had fallen to the ground, where he lay face downwards, very still.

The little party stood motionless. Mary was still unconscious. Then the detective said:

'So that's that. He's gone.'

'He was mad, I think,' said Chris sombrely. 'But he was a genius at surgery. He did a wonderful thing for Mr. Hayle's wife. Thank God we prevented him from destroying the gift he gave.'

And Martin, looking down at Mary's pale, lovely young face, peaceful now in its unconsciousness, all the lines of horror and suffering erased . . . echoed:

'Thank God!'

★   ★   ★

So ends for ever the career of Viva Rhodes; and so through the death of Basil Rhodes, self-administered, the devilish influence he had worked over her was also ended.

Mary was so weak and ill that night that Martin refused to have her driven the way back to London. He took her into Chelmsford to a comfortable hotel, only a short drive from Ashgretting, and remained there till morning.

She came round from her long swoon to find herself in a warm bed in a cosy, fire-lit bedroom, and Martin sitting beside her holding her hand. She smiled at him warmly.

'Martin,' she whispered. 'Darling, I did not give in — until I thought it was you they hurt . . . '

He fell on his knees beside her and buried his face on her breast.

'My very own,' he said brokenly, 'to think that you loved me so much . . . I am not worthy of it.'

'Nor am I worthy — of you.'

'You are everything in the world to

me,' he said passionately. 'And you are my wife. This is our real wedding-night. Try to sleep, beloved . . . forget all the horrors, and get well and strong again — for me.'

With a little sigh she shut her eyes, and with her hands clasped in his, drifted into a deep sleep.

Morning found her well again, and able to drive with her husband back to Dene Park where the Everest family awaited her with great excitement and longing.

Her beautiful face was pale and her brown eyes circled with shadows, showing the terrible mental strain through which she had passed; but when she faced her family in the familiar little drawing room at The Grange, a kind of radiant tenderness emanated from her. She looked from her father to her two sisters, to Jack, who stared wonderingly, incredulously. Then she said:

'Do you know me? It really is Mary, you know.'

'I know,' said Carol. 'I can kind of see

it now.'

'So can I — in your eyes and hair,' said Judy.

Mary gave a tremulous laugh and walked up to her father.

'Shall I show you the scar on one leg, Dad?' she asked. 'And shall I tell you of all the times we used to have when I was a child; how you spanked me one day for burning up all your pipes; how poor Mum interceded for me; how jealous I used to be because Carol, with her golden curls and big, blue eyes, was your pet?'

Old Everest cleared his throat.

'It really is Mary — my Mary!' he quavered.

'Oh, I was stupidly jealous of you all!' she said. 'I was bitter because I was ugly and out of it. That's why I ran away that Christmas morning.'

'You can't be jealous any more,' said Carol with a laugh. 'You're better-looking than any of us now.'

The sisters suddenly fell into each other's arms and kissed. Judy joined in the embrace.

'Mary — poor Mary!' said Judy.

'Not poor now,' she said, the tears running down her cheeks. 'I'm married to Martin, and you know I always wanted to marry him; so I'm rich — rich in happiness.'

'Hi, you girls!' said Martin's happy voice, 'stop kissing my wife. It's my turn!'

We do hope that you have enjoyed reading this large print book.

Did you know that all of our titles are available for purchase?

We publish a wide range of high quality large print books including:
Romances, Mysteries, Classics
General Fiction
Non Fiction and Westerns

Special interest titles available in large print are:
The Little Oxford Dictionary
Music Book, Song Book
Hymn Book, Service Book

Also available from us courtesy of Oxford University Press:
Young Readers' Dictionary
(large print edition)
Young Readers' Thesaurus
(large print edition)

For further information or a free brochure, please contact us at:
Ulverscroft Large Print Books Ltd.,
The Green, Bradgate Road, Anstey,
Leicester, LE7 7FU, England.
Tel: (00 44) **0116 236 4325**
Fax: (00 44) **0116 234 0205**

Other titles in the
Linford Romance Library:

THE LADY AT THE INN

Philippa Carey

Amanda is nineteen years old, very beautiful, very wealthy, orphaned and half-Bengali. She moves from Cal cutta to London, to live with her un- cle, but he is prejudiced against her Indian appearance and her Indian servants, so when she is abandoned at a country inn by a fortune hunter, he disowns her. The innkeeper doesn't know what to do with his distressed foreign lady guest, so he appeals for help from his landlord, the Earl of Twyford.

WORD PERFECT

Liz Harris

California, 1960s. When Londoner Leigh Carter is asked to work for Hollywood star Matt Hunter, she jumps at the chance. Down to her last dime, and soon to go home, the job's a lifesaver. But unintentionally, she humiliates Van Attwood, Matt's PA, and he resolves to pay her back, and to punish Matt for succeeding where he didn't. The arrival of Matt's truculent daughter makes things even harder, and the path to true love is far from smooth.

FINDING EDEN

Dawn Knox

18th-century London. The eldest child of a respectable watchmaker, Eva Bonner has no inkling of the catastrophic downward turn her life is about to take. Exploited, beaten, separated from her family, and wrongfully accused, she is transported to Australia as a virtual slave. Little wonder that when love finds her, she refuses to believe that it can possibly last . . .